MILLIE MAVEN
AND THE WHITE SWORD

TED DEKKER & RACHELLE DEKKER

Cover art and design by Manuel Preitano

Printed in the U.S.A.

ISBN 978-1-7335718-5-2

CHAPTER ONE

Six days had passed since I left the Shadowlands. Six joyful days since I had completed the Trial of Shadows with my friends. The days went by far too quickly. I knew there was only one trial left and it could come at any moment. All of the students knew this, and it weighed on our minds, often creeping into our conversations.

I tried to soak up as much learning as I could during the moments between. I spent long mornings with the professors, who'd become like family. Professor Tomas—the cool uncle with charisma and funny stories. Professor Claudia—the warm grandmother who smelled like fresh-baked bread and gave tight hugs. Professor Alexandria—the strict aunt who never smiled but was smarter than everyone else. And Professor Gabriel, the quirky grandfather who was always ready to smile and wink and drop wisdom into every conversation.

Graceful Dean Kyra was always around, adding comfort to any room she was in. The morning after our Trial of Shadows victory celebration, she brought me the red cloak from the Great Teacher.

As promised, Professor Alexandria had it washed but not mended. Its tattered trim seemed more beautiful than ever. I slept with the soft garment, a reminder of the Great Teacher's love for me. Of his love for everyone.

After mornings of learning, I spent afternoons running around FIGS with the other students, all of whom I now considered friends. The Shadowlands had changed us, united us, as was its purpose. Even the Elite twins had changed their ways and no longer walked around bullying smaller kids or commanding lackeys. Dash and Boomer had become close friends, which surprised Mac and me.

Doris kept mostly to herself but no longer cut anyone with sharp words. I tried a few times to offer friendly conversation, but she was evasive. She seemed hurt, as though the sting of the Shadowlands hadn't healed. And maybe it hadn't.

I knew I was called to love her, not judge her, so I practiced offering her kindness when I could without expecting anything in return.

My nights were filled with laughter. At the fireside in the common room we chatted and made up jokes and stories. We caught popcorn in our mouths, which Boomer was brilliant at, and played silly games. I tried teaching Mac to draw a simple flower. This turned out to be much harder than I thought because we spent more time giggling than drawing.

I couldn't remember, of course, but my heart wondered if I'd ever been as happy as I was during those six days. With the love of the Great Teacher flowing through me and people I adored close by, everything felt perfect.

"Millie." Mac snapped her fingers in front of my face. The noise yanked me from my dreamy state. "Earth to Millie."

We were outside, standing on the lush green grass behind the FIGS dorms. Her face was serious and I knew her competitive nature was in full bloom. At the beginning of the week, Dean Kyra had announced that a FIGS tradition would take place today: the annual FIGS relay race.

Monday we had been instructed to divide into three teams of seven, each team with the goal of getting their team flag across the finish line first. The prize was extra free time and no chores for three days. Riggs boasted that his team had won the summer he'd attended FIGS. He wore it like a badge of honor. I'd seen the spark his story ignited in Mac's eyes. She wanted that prize and the bragging rights that came with it.

It was all in good fun. A competition would have divided us before the Shadowlands, but we really were different now.

The teachers picked team captains: Adam, Gwendolyn, and Mac. Each received a colored flag and the task of choosing their teammates over the course of the week. Mac didn't pick anyone for the first two days. She'd said she was scouting to make the best possible choice. The other girls in our dorm had rolled their eyes and giggled. But when she finally asked me to be on her team, I was relieved.

"Of course I was going to ask you," she'd said. "I just didn't want anyone to think I was playing favorites."

I didn't want to disappoint her, so Thursday morning I shook off all the great memories of the week and focused.

"Get your head in the game," she said.

"Sorry," I said.

Our team had the purple flag. We huddled close as we prepared for the race's start. The other faces around me were serious. Mac and I were joined by Harvey,

Lianna, Ciara, Sid, and Polly. The only girl in our dorm not on our team was Olive, because Gwendolyn had asked her before Mac did.

"Okay, guys," Mac said. "This is the moment we've been training for."

"Wait, we were supposed to be training for this?" Polly teased.

"Yeah, I totally didn't do that," Sid echoed.

"Come on, guys!" Mac said. "Don't you want to win?"

"We're just giving you trouble," Polly said. "We're about to wipe the floor with these fools."

The others nodded and Mac smiled. "That's what I'm talking about!" she said. I smiled at their enthusiasm and had to admit I was excited as well.

The course started ten paces ahead of us and followed the shape of a large oval much larger than I could see. It covered most of the FIGS grounds and had different layers of difficulty. Yesterday Dean Kyra gave us a map and the rules so we could determine which team member would do each leg of the race. It started with a long stretch of lawn that bled into the forest, cut across a section of water, went over a small hill, through a dense stand of trees, across the FIGS amphitheater, and finally finished at the line ten paces behind us.

"Students," a booming voice called from the north side of the pathway.

We turned to see Dean Kyra joined by the professors and Leads. Dean Kyra smiled. "Welcome to the annual FIGS relay race. This is one of my favorite events of the summer!"

She motioned toward the starting line. "Your first relay member will start on this line after the others have taken their places at the corresponding handoff points. As you know, gifts are permitted, so use them well."

She turned and motioned toward the finish line. "The first colored flag across that line will join the ranks of FIGS relay race champions. Remember, there are only two rules. First, you are not allowed to use your gift to harm another runner. Breaking this rule will disqualify your entire team. Second, every player on your team must compete."

She smiled, a twinkle in her eye. "We will begin momentarily, so give your teammates your best words of encouragement and then get to your places!"

Nervous energy swirled in my belly.

"Hey, purple team!" someone snarked a few yards away. A voice I knew well. I turned to see Boomer standing with the green team, led by Gwendolyn, his eyes ready for playful confrontation.

"Ready for our takedown?" Boomer tossed out.

His teammate Dash spoke up. "Dude, a takedown is when the other team takes *you* down. We don't want them to take *us* down."

"Oh," Boomer said. Then back to us. "You ready to be taken *down*?!"

I chuckled as Mac rolled her eyes. Lianna opened her mouth, but Mac raised her hand to demand silence. "No fraternizing with the enemy," she said. "Let's go over the lineup again."

Lianna and I shared a look, trying not to burst into giggles. Mac was taking this very seriously.

"I'm first," Harvey said. "Across the lawn to the forest's edge."

"Then to me," Lianna said. "I'm small but quick through the trees. I'll pass it to Ciara."

The girl nodded. "And I'll continue until I hand it off to Sid."

"And I'll turn the water to ice and slide across," Sid said.

"To me," Mac said. "I'll head over the hill, clearing obstacles between me and Millie."

"And then you'll follow me along the outside of the course using your gift to help me if I need it," I said.

"You're sure that's legal?" Lianna asked her.

"There are only two rules," Mac reminded. "And

helping Millie doesn't break either of them."

We all nodded. It was a good plan. I didn't have a gift like the others. I wasn't sure I was ever going to get one, and when I thought about it too long I started to doubt my worth again. I tried not to think about that and focused on what I did know: the Great Teacher had chosen me for something, and I was supposed to be here. That was all I needed to understand.

"I'll move through the trees to the amphitheater," I said. "Handing off the flag to—"

"Me," Polly finished. "And I'll use my speed to book it across the finish line." She rubbed her hands together excitedly. "I hope Adam tries to race me. I've been practicing."

Mac chuckled and extended her hand to the middle of our huddle. "Hands in," she said. We all put our palms in the middle and waited for her cue.

"Purple team for the win on three," Mac said and counted us up to three.

"Purple team for the win!" we cheered, throwing our hands into the air.

My best friend's enthusiasm was infectious and suddenly I wanted the victory. We parted as we moved to the checkpoints along the course, where either a professor or Lead had been stationed. Mac gave my hand a squeeze as we split, and I cut through the trees toward my mark.

"Of course," a voice said behind me. I turned to see Doris walking through the trees behind me. "Fate just won't let us be, will it?" She was on the green team with Boomer and her twin, Dash.

"You're running this leg of the race too?" I asked.

"Lucky us," Doris said. Her eyes looked tired and her face paler than usual. She stumbled on a tree root and nearly fell. I moved to catch her, but as she straightened, she pulled away.

"Are you okay?" I asked.

"I'm fine," she said. "Ready to kick your butt." Her words were playful but her tone was short and strained. Worry pricked at my heart.

I thought to prod but couldn't before a third student joined us. Gwendolyn.

"Well, well," she said. "Battle of the ladies. I like it."

"You won't when I squash you," Doris teased.

"Oh, I'm looking forward to watching you try," Gwendolyn teased back.

I smiled and relaxed a bit as they bantered. Doris seemed more comfortable when it wasn't just the two of us.

We reached our checkpoint and found Riggs

propped against a tree. "You girls ready?" he asked.

We nodded and took our places beside him.

He glanced at his watch. "Fifteen seconds," he said.

I took a deep breath and shook my head clear. I couldn't be distracted and blow this for my team. Mac would kill me.

"Ten seconds," Riggs said.

Focus, Millie. You may not have a gift, but you'll have Mac. You can do this.

"Five, four, three, two," Riggs counted. A loud shot announced the race had started. From all of Mac's planning I knew the course was almost half a mile. Seven hundred seventy-two yards to be exact. Mac knew the length of each section.

"You only have to run the length of a football field," Mac had said. "That's all."

I'd never seen a football field, but I told myself I could do it. It was just a football field . . . covered in dense, forested terrain. Doris and Gwendolyn were bigger and faster than I was. I swallowed my nerves and ignored the weight fear poured into my feet. They were filled with lead.

We waited in silence, each caught up in her own thoughts. From the corner of my eye I noticed Doris waver a bit. She didn't look well at all. I thought to check again but Riggs said, "Here they come."

I turned to see three figures racing down the hill at our backs. Dash was in the lead, Mac closely behind. Olive brought up the rear.

"Come on, Olive!" Gwendolyn encouraged.

Doris smirked as Dash reached us and was the first one to hand off his team's flag. She snatched it and took off as Dash placed his hands on his knees and exhaled heavily.

Then Mac was next to me, purple flag extended, hair wild in the wind. "Go, Millie!"

I grabbed the flag and chased Doris. I saw Mac rush to the outskirts of the course. I tried to stay as close to the outside line as I could. Only five yards stood between us as we moved. She was essentially running two sections of the course because I didn't have a gift. But I couldn't think about that or it would slow me down.

The terrain was rocky and uneven, thick with roots and overgrowth. Its knitted trees weren't easy to navigate.

"I got you, Millie!" Mac yelled. Directly in front of me was a wide thicket of thorn bushes that stood to my knees. I started to slow but Mac created a path through the threat so I could pass easily.

I smiled at her and pushed my legs faster. We had to win this.

"Not fair!" Gwendolyn yelled from behind, but I ignored her. I didn't look back. I just cranked forward. I could see Doris's long black ponytail flipping as she navigated the path at least ten paces ahead. She was fast. I needed to be faster.

I dropped my focus into another gear and prayed my body could give what I needed to beat her. The space between us started to lessen. I was faster than I thought, or maybe Doris was losing her strength.

The second proved to be true. I watched her quick sprint slow to a jog. Another warning bell rang in my mind, but I knew this was my moment to surpass her.

"Go, Millie, go!" Mac yelled.

I was nearly to Doris when she slowed to a stop, swayed as if the breeze pushed her, and collapsed. I changed course and went straight to her. Something was wrong.

"Millie!" Mac cried.

Gwendolyn took the lead as I dropped to my knees.

"Doris," I said. She was lying on her side, face white as a sheet and covered in red splotches, sweat sparkling across her forehead.

"Millie, what are you doing?" Mac yelled.

"Doris," I tried again, shaking the girl slightly. No response.

"Mac, get help!" I cried. I glanced up at her through the trees. "Now, Mac! Something is wrong!"

Mac looked disappointed but rushed back toward the point where I hoped Riggs was still stationed. Several strands of Doris's long black hair had fallen loose from her ponytail and lay across her cheeks. I brushed them back. That's when I noticed the cakey residue under her eyes. Makeup?

Yes, covered in powder to hide it well. But sweat had made it slide away. Underneath were dark puffy circles. Dread dropped into my gut. I had seen these dark circles before. I'd had them myself in the Shadow-lands.

Impossible, I thought. *There must be some other explanation.* But even as the sound of pounding feet reentered my awareness, my heart already knew Doris was in trouble.

The kind brought on by worm sludge.

CHAPTER TWO

They came quickly for Doris. Mac and Riggs were followed by Professor Tomas and Dean Kyra. Doris was responsive, so they took her to Professor Gabriel. The relay race was postponed, which made some kids angry until news spread how seriously ill Doris was.

Then we all just worried. An hour passed as we waited for news. I wanted to tell Dean Kyra that I thought maybe Doris had found a way into the dungeons and gotten her hands on worm sludge. If she had, we might all be in terrible danger. If Doris had ignored Dean Kyra's stern warning and wrote in the dungeon's book of history, all of FIGS could be destroyed. The thought made me cringe.

But puffy eyes and dark circles could be attributed to a lot of things. I was afraid I might be overreacting.

In the Shadowlands no one had passed out from eating worm sludge. Doris was just sick and didn't need me complicating things by jumping to conclusions. Besides, Dean Kyra had said they'd sealed the dungeons, so how could Doris have gone there?

We were all in the lower-level common area when Dean Kyra entered. Mac and I were slouched on one of the yellow couches. We sat up quickly as all eyes turned to the dean.

Dash moved to her side, and the kind woman placed a hand on his shoulder. "It's alright, Mr. Elite," she said. "She's going to be alright."

"What's wrong with her?" Gwendolyn asked. She'd been crying and her eyes were red. She felt guilty for rushing past us during the race instead of stopping to make sure her friend wasn't hurt. Ciara was comforting her.

"She's contracted an unidentified illness," Dean Kyra said.

"Unidentified?" Dash asked.

"That sounds bad," Adam said.

"It simply means unknown and uncommon," Dean Kyra said.

"That doesn't really make it sound better," Adam said.

"Can't Professor Gabriel heal her?" Boomer asked.

"He's working on it," Dean Kyra answered. "He's with her now."

"It's taking a long time." Fear filled Adam's eyes.

"I know you're worried about your friend," Dean Kyra said. "But we're doing everything we can to help Miss Elite recover quickly. Until we know more, we're moving her into a private room where she can rest."

"You mean away from us," Boomer said. "In case it's contagious."

"Oh man, oh man," Mac whispered beside me, shaking her head.

"Is it contagious?" Boomer asked.

Whispers and concern started to ripple through the group.

"Please, students," Dean Kyra said, raising her hand. "We're taking every precaution for your safety. We'll figure this out and everything will be alright."

"Can I see her?" Dash asked. I'd never heard his voice so thin and scared.

Dean Kyra's smile held empathy for the boy. "I'm sorry, dear Dash, but not until we're certain it's safe."

I could tell he was fighting back tears.

"As soon as I know more, I'll tell you," Dean Kyra continued. "For now, the best thing you can do for

Doris is try to go about your days as normal. She wouldn't want any of you to worry."

With that Dean Kyra gave Dash's shoulder a squeeze and left us. The sense in the room was heavy and silent. I tried not to imagine a worst-case scenario. Mac and I returned to the couch, Boomer joining us.

"Poor Dash," Boomer whispered.

I offered him a small smile. "It's going to be okay," I said, placing my hand on Boomer's forearm.

"Really?" he asked.

I wanted to tell him and Mac about my suspicions, but their worried faces suggested my thoughts would only make things worse. So I kept them to myself. Dean Kyra and the other professors were dealing with Doris. Everything would be fine.

"Yes," I said as much for myself as for Boomer.

But my mind kept asking, *What if I'm wrong?*

✦

Doris.

The voice calling her name woke her. Doris's eyes flickered open to a dark room. Shapes started to materialize as her eyes adjusted. She wasn't in her dorm. She sat up and regretted it. Her body ached and the movement hurt every muscle. Doris took a few deep breaths as the pain subsided.

She was in a plain room that reminded her of a patient's hospital room. She reached over to flick on the bedside table lamp. The small wooden clock at the lamp's base read 2:15 a.m. Doris pulled back the heavy white blanket and slowly placed her feet on the cold floor.

She was shaky and weak. Her head pounded and her stomach turned. She could faintly remember the professors hovering over her, trying to figure out what was wrong. Doris closed her eyes and swallowed through the pain. She could have told them if she'd been able to speak.

Doris. The haunting voice came again. The same voice that always came. The one she feared and desired. He gave her what she craved most.

Worm sludge.

She needed more. The vial he gave her most recently had only lasted four days. She'd tried to take as little as she could, but she needed to consume the small doses more often. Just enough to take the edge off. To quiet her mind.

He'd promised her more but she didn't know what he would require in return. Doris had tried to fight the urge for the last two days, but it had become so strong. She couldn't live without it. She didn't know how. And she hated herself for it.

He was right about her. She was weak and she needed him. Like a beetle, he'd crawled into her brain and taken up residence. He wouldn't leave her alone, and though she feared him, she needed him to stay.

Come, Doris.

Tears filled her eyes. She didn't want to go. She didn't want to be this way. But she was and she would.

Doris stood on shaky legs and left the private room. Quietly she followed the voice from the third floor into the main entryway, across the open space, through the double doors, and toward the dungeon's locked door.

Her feet knew where they were going. He was in her mind, leading her there. The door had been bolted from the inside. She'd found herself daydreaming about different ways to break in. Her best idea was to change the form of the lock with her gift while no one was looking.

The worm sludge was always on her mind, distracting her in class and calling her back to it with every free moment. The powder in the golden vial, which Millie had brought down from the mountain in the Trial of Shadows, had freed her from the goop but then abandoned her.

But he had never abandoned her. He wouldn't leave her alone.

Soren. The one who'd worked his way into her mind.

The first time he called to her was when they were in the Shadowlands. While the rest slept, she followed his voice and met him in the marsh. She knew of Soren from Millie, but her mind had already been clouded by then.

He told her where to find more goop and she'd led the others there. He convinced Doris she was saving them. Offering them power and freedom. Instead he trapped them in a curse. And she couldn't be rid of it because without it she hated herself too much.

He called her again the night they returned to FIGS. Millie had nearly caught her talking with him outside the dungeon door. He'd given her a bottle of slime and promised her more.

She'd wanted to refuse but wasn't strong enough. She considered telling someone, asking for help, but they'd take it from her! She both wanted and feared this. Her mind was a constant tangle of revulsion and desire.

Now, as Doris stood there staring at the locked door, part of her hoped someone would walk in and stop her, because she couldn't stop herself.

Slowly Doris heard the bolt on the inside of the door slide back. Her heart raced as the knob twisted on its own and the thick wooden panel creaked open a few inches. Pulse racing, Doris pushed the door open and saw the empty descending stairs. A shiver ran the length of her spine as she glanced around.

She appeared to be alone but she knew his presence was there.

Come, Doris.

She stepped through the door and down the narrow stone steps. Torches jutted from the walls, lighting her way. She stepped into the domed atrium and approached the double doors. They unlocked of their own accord and popped open. Doris took short labored breaths. The battle raged inside as she lifted a torch from the wall and headed through.

The tunnels were darker than she remembered. The aroma of sweet sludge filled her nostrils and gave her goosebumps. She went down the stone passageway about five paces, toward the prison doors.

"Doris," Soren's voice said. He came into focus ahead of her, looking different than she remembered. In the Shadowlands he'd come dressed in a long dark cloak, hood pulled up over his head so that shadows hid most of his face. Here he looked like a simple woodsman.

"I know I look different," he said. "I wanted to present myself in a more approachable way."

"Why?" Doris mustered.

"Because I don't want you to be afraid, Doris," the woodsman said.

But Doris was still very afraid.

"Come with me," Soren said. "I'll give you what you crave."

He turned toward a door, pushed it open, and stepped inside. Doris followed, even as her legs trembled. Inside she found a desk. A book, an ink jar, and a quill sat on top. Something in her heart warned her that nothing good could come from this. But she needed more sludge, and Soren had it.

She looked up at the woodsman. "What is this place?"

"This is where I make you more beautiful," he said.

Doris was struck by his words.

"Isn't that what you want? What you really desire?" Soren said. "You wish to be better so people will love you. So your mother will love you."

The word "mother" made Doris's heart ache. She couldn't remember her mother, but something in her soul knew there was darkness between them. She did long to be better. She did long for her mother's love.

Tears filled her eyes. "You can make me beautiful?"

"Yes, Doris. I offered the same path to Millie, but she

refused to see the truth." Soren placed a kind hand on her shoulder. "I should have known you were the one who'd be wise enough to accept."

Warmth filled Doris's body and some of the fear lifted from her chest. Her skin seemed to buzz and she glanced down to see it was almost shimmering. She gasped and held her hands in front of her face. She turned them over in awe. She looked so alive.

"Would you like to see?" the woodsman asked.

He withdrew a small square mirror from his pocket and handed it to Doris. She grasped it and held it out to see her face. What reflected back was stunning. Her skin, eyes, lips, all were still hers but more beautiful than she could have imagined.

More of her fear subsided. He had done what he promised. Maybe he wasn't so terrible. How could someone who had created such beauty be terrible?

"Do you like it?" he asked.

"Yes," Doris replied.

"I could make all of FIGS this way. Beautiful."

Without removing her eyes from her own reflection Doris said, "But isn't FIGS already beautiful?"

"Not as beautiful as I could make it," Soren said. "Millie let me down, but you could help me. They'll see your beauty and want the same for themselves. I'll gladly provide it. Then they'll love you."

His words sang to her desires. That was all she wanted. To be loved and to not feel worthless.

"All you have to do is write in the book," Soren said.

Doris drew her eyes from her reflection and glanced at the book on the desk. It was a simple brown leather-bound book with the words *Book of History* inscribed on the front. Doris recalled Dean Kyra's dire warning never to write in the book. Her heart rate quickened.

Soren moved to the opposite side of the desk and pulled back the single chair. He patted the seat, ushering Doris to come sit. Her feet moved against the warning in her heart. But she wanted to be beautiful. She wanted to be loved.

Doris sat, staring at the book and feeling the presence of Soren behind her. He leaned down so his lips were only inches from her ear. "Tell me what you are without beauty," he said, his voice low.

"Worthless," Doris whispered.

"Do you want to be worthless?"

"No." Tears gathered, blurring Doris's vision of the book.

Soren reached around Doris and opened the cover. "You can change that. You can do what Millie couldn't."

"Will people get hurt?" Doris asked.

"When making a thing new and beautiful,

sometimes you have to burn down the old so beauty can rise from the ashes. But the end result is a treasure beyond imagination."

A tear slipped down Doris's cheek. Emotion ravaged her throat. Dean Kyra's warning voice was growing. What if Soren was lying? But he promised beauty to everyone. And beauty couldn't be evil? Right?

Soren lifted the quill and held it out to her. Trembling, Doris looked at it in Soren's hands. Part of her wanted to stop. Part of her knew deep down that writing in the book would betray everyone. But a larger part of her wanted what Millie had rejected. She wanted the love Soren promised.

"Write in the book, Doris," Soren said. "Write and be my Judas."

Doris lifted her hand and reached for the quill. She hesitated, her fingertips nearly touching the feather. Soren placed it in her hand and guided it to the blank page that lay before her. "Write these words," he murmured in her ear. He whispered a single statement, slow and firm.

The end of the quill touched the page and black ink bled into it. Dread sat in her gut as she contemplated what she was writing. *But he made me beautiful*, she thought again. *He would do that with FIGS too. Right?*

The quill and her hand became one. She wrote the same sentence once, twice, three times.

"Write it again," Soren said.

Doris did. Over and over. As the words appeared on the paper, Doris's hand started to quiver. She could feel something electric filling her blood, rolling up her arm and across her shoulders. The power flashed down her spine and filled her chest as her hand flew over the page, writing word after word.

Soon the page was filled from top to bottom with the same line of text. Text she had written. Words she knew would change everything. She whispered them softly as she wrote it again.

"I give Soren authority to enter FIGS and do his will."

"Good," Soren's voice vibrated around her as her eyes stayed trained on the page, hand continuing to write. "Let us begin."

She was certain of only one thing: she was working with Soren. And because she was working with him, everything was about to change.

Chapter Three

I struggled to sleep as I worried about Doris. Once in the night I woke and pulled out the white journal Dean Kyra had given me. The cover was in shadows, but I could make out the cross in the thin moonlight that filtered in through the window. I hoped to find some guidance or wisdom on its pages, but the book was still blank. I reminded myself of what Dean Kyra had said: when the student was ready, the teacher would come.

I held the journal close to my chest as I fell back asleep. But when I woke up, the dread was still with me. It lived with me all through the morning as I got ready. I couldn't shake it. It appeared that most of my classmates were suffering from similar unease.

Perhaps that's why at breakfast Dean Kyra announced we would have morning class outside in the old amphitheater. Doris was still in bed ill, and the professors hadn't discovered anything new about her condition. A change of scenery might do us good.

After we finished eating I joined Mac and Boomer and we headed for the open-air auditorium. I'd never been there before and didn't even know it existed until the relay.

All the professors except for Gabriel, who had offered to stay close to Doris, walked with us to the amphitheater. It sat in a large clearing behind trees that hid it from view of the school.

Though the semi-circular stone walls towered over thirty feet high, the structure was small and humble compared to pictures I'd seen of ancient amphitheaters. We entered under an arch and I saw rows of seating stacked to the top of the walls facing a simple stone stage. It wouldn't have been anything special except everything was covered in plants—every row of seats, every inch of ground, all the way to the stage and behind. Foliage bloomed.

My mouth opened in surprise. From the outside I could not have guessed such beauty existed within. A dozen or so small statues in different positions stood along the inside perimeter. Aged by weather and green moss, stone children ran, laughed, and played.

"We call it the Children's Garden," Professor Tomas said as we walked in.

The effect was stunning. Flowers bloomed in every color and size. Ivy blossomed and climbed. A small grove of lemon trees grew to the left of the stage while several huge oaks towered behind it. Birds perched on the theater's stone walls and on the statues of children, singing to one another. Butterflies fluttered around the flowers, and bees buzzed, happily doing their work.

"Everything always grows so well here," Professor Claudia said. "There's something powerful in the soil."

"What are these statues?" someone asked.

"They have stood here as long as FIGS," Professor Claudia said. "Many believe they are an ode to the students."

"They say the Great Teacher himself carved them," Professor Alexandria said.

"This is one of many gardens here at FIGS," Dean Kyra said, coming in last. I turned to see her eyeing me. "Some more ravishing than others." She gave me a small wink and I knew she was referring to my garden experience.

Yes, this garden was beautiful, but nothing would ever compare to the garden of the Great Teacher. I wondered if I would ever get to see it again.

"I can feel the soil here," Mac whispered to my right. Dean Kyra must have overheard.

"Me too," she said to Mac.

"This place holds great significance for FIGS," Dean Kyra said.

"Why?" Mac asked.

Dean Kyra and Professor Claudia shared a knowing look.

"This is the site of the Great Teacher's sacrifice," the motherly professor said.

"What do you mean?" Polly asked. All the students turned their eyes to Professor Claudia.

"This is where the Great Teacher offered his life in exchange for the freedom of his students. In the beginning, when he roamed the school halls, he called each child here by name. He loved each one dearly. But then the darkness came and convinced the beloved children to turn against him."

I remembered this story from my first day at FIGS. Dean Kyra had told it to me in the library right before she gave me the Great Teacher's journal. We had all heard bits of the story by now, through classes and in our own discussions about FIGS. We all knew the Great Teacher had been killed.

"I thought the kids murdered him," Boomer said.

"They did kill him, but only because he gave his life so they could be freed from the darkness of fear."

"That happened here?" Mac asked.

Claudia looked around fondly. "Yes, and the power

of his sacrifice, the power of his blood that soaked the ground, lives on in the soil."

"How do you know the Great Teacher isn't still dead?" Dash asked.

"That's the power of his story," Dean Kyra said. "Even in death the Great Teacher lives."

"But if no one has seen him, how do you know?" Dash pressed.

"Because you can feel him," I said.

Eyes shifted to me and I saw Dean Kyra smile in my direction.

"Yes," the dean said. Then back to Dash. "You have to have faith, Mr. Elite."

Dash's face took on a pondering look and the students fell quiet.

"This is one of the reasons we wanted to hold class here this morning," Dean Kyra said. "Because of the power in the ground itself."

"Find an open seat," Professor Alexandria said. "Quickly." We turned toward the stadium seating and maneuvered around the flowers to find spaces where the stone seats weren't covered in plants.

As we situated ourselves, Dean Kyra took center stage. I loved when Dean Kyra led the class. The other professors stood behind her.

"You have heard me say many times that FIGS's

primary purpose is to teach you each about the power you possess," Dean Kyra started. "I'm not referring to the physical gifts you believe make you special, but rather the power of your hearts."

She placed her hands behind her back and started pacing. "As we near the third and final trial, understanding your true purpose will be critical for finishing strong."

"What is the third trial?" Polly asked.

"You will know when it is upon you," Dean Kyra answered. I couldn't help but smile. I was getting used to her answering in ways that didn't actually tell us anything.

"Hear me, please," she continued. "This is a lesson of the heart that will forever impact your life. Whatever you do in fear breeds more fear, but all actions done in love will result in more love. Offer love to the things you fear because love casts out fear."

I felt the Great Teacher's warmth spring up in my heart. I had felt him often since the Trial of Shadows. He was with me always and this truth made me smile.

"You all faced deep darkness and fear in the first two trials," Dean Kyra said. "But your journeys aren't finished. And what you will face next will change you. But if you can remember this simple truth—that fighting fear with fear will only bring you suffering—I promise you will thrive."

Dean Kyra smiled at us.

"And in all things, *love*. Whether that be loving yourself, others, or even the circumstances you find yourself in. Love will always cast out fear. For there is no fear in love."

She looked each of us in the eye.

"Do you understand?" she asked.

No one answered for a moment, then Boomer said what most of us were probably thinking. "Honestly, not really."

Other students giggled and I saw wide smiles on the professors.

"But I'm willing to bet that after the third trial I will," Boomer finished.

This brought laughter from even the teachers. For a moment the garden filled with joy.

I sensed Doris before I could see her. All the little hairs on the back of my neck stood up. I turned my head toward the entry arch and a moment later she walked under it.

She strode in looking much better than she had yesterday. Her skin seemed to shimmer and I was struck by how beautiful she looked. I thought I could see tears in her eyes, though, which triggered a silent warning in my heart. Everyone but Dean Kyra was still caught up in giggling and enjoying the day. She also noticed Doris and turned her head toward the girl, concerned.

That caught the attention of Professor Alexandria, who looked shocked and afraid at Doris's sudden arrival. Gradually everyone noticed the seemingly healed girl as she walked toward the center of the theater, eyes locked on Dean Kyra and the professors.

"Doris!" Dash stood, smiling. "You look so much better!"

Doris stole a slight glance toward him and offered a small smile. "I feel beautiful," she said. Her voice was small and strained. The warning in my heart grew. Something was not right.

Her attention shifted back to the teachers and Dean Kyra approached.

"Doris, what are you doing out of bed?" Dean Kyra asked. I could hear the suspicion in her tone. She knew something was off too.

"I had to come," Doris said, her voice low and trembling, "to make things beautiful."

"Come, I can take you back," Dean Kyra said.

Doris was shaking her head.

"Come now," Dean Kyra said, stepping off the stage.

"No!" Doris snapped. "This is the only way."

"What's going on?" Dash asked as he left his seat.

"Stay where you are, Mr. Elite," Dean Kyra ordered.

Dash looked confused. Students began to stand up.

"Everyone, stay where you are!" Professor Alexandria boomed.

"When making something new and beautiful, sometimes you have to burn down the old," Doris said.

"You've been deceived," Dean Kyra said. "Whatever he promised you is a lie. Let me help you."

"No, it's too late," Doris said.

"What did you do?" Dean Kyra asked. It was the first time I'd heard her sound afraid.

"I wrote in the *Book of History*," Doris said.

As if someone flipped a switch, the sky filled with dark clouds and the air dropped ten degrees. A harsh wind whipped across the Children's Garden, rustling the flowers and bending the trees. Lightning cracked the sky and thunder shook the ground. I looked up and saw a vicious storm brewing behind the clouds. She'd written in the *Book of History*. What did that mean?

Professor Claudia started to scream and I saw Doris approaching the teachers. Black fog, thick and coiled, started oozing from her fingertips and spreading across the ground toward them. Quick and threatening, it snaked like veins over the dirt until it formed a thick knitted covering.

The blanket of fog destroyed everything in its path. Flowers and roots quickly turned to dust. The heavy wind whipped the dust away, leaving no clue anything had ever been there.

"Run!" Professor Alexandria yelled.

"No!" Dean Kyra countered. "Do not resist!"

But Professor Alexandria was quaking with fear. "Run back to the school! Run now!"

Panic broke out among the students as we stumbled from our seats. The wind knocked me to my knees and I collided with Mac, who had been standing beside me. We tumbled down several steps and landed in a heap, my head slamming against the hard dirt.

I rolled away, dizzy, and pushed myself back up to standing. Mac found her feet too, fear and panic coursing across her face. The other students rushed down the steps and out through the arch. Mac and I were nearly through the arch ourselves when I saw the horrifying darkness coming from Doris capture Professor Alexandria as she tried to flee.

It wrapped around her ankles and crawled up her legs, pulling her to the ground and dragging her back to center stage. At the same time, the fog attacked Professor Tomas and Professor Claudia as they tried to use their gifts against the intensifying darkness.

The black fog didn't even flinch. The professors' gifts failed them, and the darkness cocooned all three teachers in coiling tendrils. I didn't want to watch but I couldn't look away. I was frozen in terror beside Mac as the professors vanished.

They were gone. Nowhere to be seen. Taken by the fog.

"Oh no . . ." Mac's words failed. We still couldn't move as the fog towered over Doris and continued to spread, rising up the amphitheater seating, turning all to dust. It turned its attention to Dean Kyra.

"No!" I screamed.

The fog stilled as Doris turned her head slowly to look at me. Her eyes were bright in the mist, but the veins under her shimmering skin were dark and I knew the darkness flowed through her entire body. Doris wasn't alone. Something was with her.

Someone.

Soren.

Fear stole my breath.

"Millie, you must go!" Dean Kyra yelled. The wind yanked her silver braid across her face.

Doris snapped her head back toward the dean, ready to attack.

"Millie, come on!" Mac screamed, grabbing my arm and yanking it. My feet stumbled as we moved out of the Children's Garden. My mind was a wreck. Emotion balled in my throat. I couldn't leave Dean Kyra, I just couldn't. I pulled free from Mac's hold and turned back.

"Millie!" Mac cried. But I stepped back into the garden just in time to see Dean Kyra surround herself in a brilliant ball of light and vanish from the stage. I didn't know whether to be worried or relieved.

Again Doris turned toward me. The black fog hovered at her back and flowed from her fingers. Doris drilled me with a dark stare and I knew I was looking at Soren behind her eyes. I was afraid, but I was angry too.

"I see you, Soren," I yelled over the harsh winds. "What did you do to Doris?"

"Exactly what she asked me to," Doris said, but it wasn't her. The voice was hollow and deep. It was coming from her mouth but it belonged to Soren.

"You'll never win. Light will always beat the darkness!"

"And where's your light now?"

I could feel my fear threatening to kill my faith, but I knew the Great Teacher was with me. He said he always was.

"The Great Teacher has abandoned you," Doris said with Soren's voice. "Now I'll destroy you all and turn FIGS to dust."

Doris moved toward me. Darkness flowed behind her and Soren's voice spilled from her mouth.

"I'm going to start with you, Millie Maven."

Chapter Four

Soren's threat chilled me to the core. As I turned to run, a thick cord of black fog burst from Doris's palm and came directly for my chest. Had I been a half second faster I might have evaded it.

The dark coil slammed into my heart. Massive pressure exploded across my chest and knocked me into the air. I flew backward five yards and smashed into the ground at Mac's feet.

All the wind escaped my mouth and I grunted from the heavy fall. The spot over my heart burned as I finally sucked in a breath and rolled to my side.

"Millie," Mac said, dropping to my aid. "Get up, Millie! We have to go."

I coughed and let her help me to my feet. Doris was picking herself up off the ground as well. She'd been knocked down? How? Why?

There wasn't time for questions because she was getting back up and quickly.

"Come on!" Mac cried, still gripping my arm. We ran toward FIGS, which loomed against the raging sky.

The wind's violence increased and pushed against us as we ran with all our might. Our feet hit the main graveled path lined with oaks and we carried on toward the school.

"We have to find the others!" I yelled against the thrashing wind.

Mac and I hurried and soon burst through the main entry. The school was dark and quiet. We were breathing heavily, and our ragged breaths echoed in the marbled hall.

"Where are they?" I asked.

"Hey! Anyone!" Mac called out.

My chest burned again and I reached inside my shirt to place my hand over my heart. My fingers touched the surface of my medallion and I yanked it out. It was hot to the touch and was scorched directly in the center. My shirt was burned as well but my skin was fine, bruised but intact.

I held my medallion and felt its power course through me. It had saved me from a Soren-sized blast. It had protected me.

"I found them!" someone cried over the banister. Mac and I glanced up to see Lianna motioning for us to come. We raced for the stairs and took them two at a time as the small girl disappeared. We rounded the top of the stairs and headed for the second-level common area beside the lecture halls.

Mac took the lead, stepping into the room with me on her heels. Everyone was there unloading a cabinet filled with weapons. They held swords, knives, a crossbow, and more. Dash stood on a long table they had pushed up to the case and was retrieving the items from behind the broken glass.

"What are you doing?" Mac asked.

"Defending ourselves," Dash said, handing Boomer an ax.

"Where are the professors?" Olive asked us. "Did they go for help?"

Students stared at us, waiting for an explanation, and I couldn't find the words to explain what we'd seen.

"They're gone," Mac said.

"As in dead?" Boomer said.

Mac and I just stood there in silence because we didn't know. They were just gone.

"Another reason to defend ourselves," Dash said, picking up the pace.

"From your sister?" Mac asked.

Dash snapped his head toward Mac. "That was not my sister. That was something else."

"But it's using your sister," Mac said. "You're going to hurt her or yourselves."

"Dean Kyra said not to resist," I offered.

"Did you see that thing?" Polly cried.

"We're going to die, aren't we?" Lianna whimpered.

"I can't believe they actually have weapons in the school," I said. I recalled Mac telling me these weapons were here, but I'd never ventured into this room to see them for myself.

"Riggs told me they're relics from generations back when teachers used them for training. They've been stored in this display for decades now," Adam explained, taking a sword from Dash.

"Do you even know how to use them?" Mac asked.

"We'll learn fast," Adam said.

"I don't want to die," Lianna whimpered again.

"We aren't going to die," Polly said, loading the crossbow she held. "We're going to kill it."

"Kill it! Are you insane?" Mac cried.

"You can't kill Soren," I said.

The room stopped and all eyes turned to me.

"Soren is controlling my sister?" Dash asked.

I swallowed. "I'm pretty sure."

"Are you sure or pretty sure?" Dash demanded.

"I'm sure. And I've faced him. I don't think you can kill him with a sword."

"Then what do we do, Millie?" Boomer asked.

Again the room waited for me to answer but I didn't know what to say. I had no idea how to defeat him, but something about fighting fear with fear kept replaying in my mind. My gut was telling me this wasn't the way. Dash huffed and grabbed the last of the weapons from behind the broken glass.

"We go with plan A then," he said, jumping down from the table, a curved combat knife in hand. "We kill it."

"Maybe this is a bad idea?" Boomer said.

"It's darkness, or fog—or whatever," Mac sputtered. "How are you going to attack it with weapons?"

"It's all we have, Mac! We're just kids. We haven't mastered our gifts. What else are we supposed to do?" Dash faced off with Mac and I could see him fighting back tears. He was as terrified as the rest, just trying to find a solution.

I hadn't considered how difficult it must have been to see his twin sister in the state she was in. I couldn't blame him for wanting to fight back. But I knew in my heart it was the wrong path.

Mac said nothing and Dash strode past her, the

armed students following. We went down the stairs and back outside. The storm raged on worse than before. We pushed through the harsh wind, down FIGS's front steps, and onto the graveled path.

Through the wind I saw tendrils of darkness slithering up the hill toward FIGS. They destroyed everything they touched. Ash and dust from the ravaged earth filled the air.

Doris appeared, cresting the small hill and walking directly toward us. Her skin was starting to flake off like pieces of tissue paper torn away by the wind.

"Doris!" Dash started running for her, armed and ready.

"Dash, no!" Polly called. But the brother was desperate to save his sister and my heart lurched.

A blanket of black fog covered everything behind Doris in darkness. Soren spread out like a disease. I watched as Doris staggered and then collapsed just before reaching the gravel path. The moment her body hit the dirt, it dissipated into thousands of powdery flakes that littered the earth.

"No!" Dash screamed.

Doris had turned to dust. I noticed that this was different from the professors, who had been taken by the darkness, swallowed whole. Soren's darkness didn't need Doris anymore. A thick black cloud rose from where Doris had fallen. It grew to more than twenty feet tall, darker than the waste it left behind, and formed a figure. Not a man, but a faceless being. A fog beast that struck at us with coils like claws and fangs of venomous darkness.

Dash drew back his knife and charged the monster. The others joined him in the siege. Weapons were drawn, war cries sounded, and the group ran toward the shifting dark figure, ready to fight.

We couldn't fight Soren! Not like this.

Dash was the first to plunge his weapon into the cloudy black form, but when he tried to withdraw his weapon, the fog wrapped around his knife and yanked him off his feet. Then Soren pulled Dash into the massive dark cloud. With a shriek the boy disappeared.

Polly loosed an arrow form her crossbow into the darkness. Adam attacked next, sword raised. A coil shot out from the cloud and swallowed Polly's arrow while simultaneously snapping Adam's sword in half. Then Soren spat Dash out, tossing him through the air fifty feet to the ground.

The boy slammed against the dirt like a rag doll and lay deathly still.

It all happened in seconds. With the quick defeat of the leaders, the attack crumbled into chaos. Screaming, charging, and thrashing, desperate to protect themselves from the darkness, each one of my friends pressed in. But the harder they fought, the larger the cloud grew and the faster it came.

Like lightning strikes, tendrils of heavy black fog shot from its core and attacked the students. Soren fired sleek black arrows across the lawn at fleeing kids. One pierced Polly between her shoulder blades and she collapsed.

A tendril shaped like a sword sliced at Adam and knocked him to the ground. Soren devoured the students' weapons and used them to fight back. Dean Kyra's words floated through my brain.

Do not resist.

Our attack was only making it stronger.

Lightning struck an oak tree. The loud crack cut through the madness as the bark split and ignited. Mac snatched my hand and yanked me away. We ran down the gravel path and then cut through the row of oak trees, heading toward the forest north of the school. Beyond it was the camp where we'd had our Initiation Trial. The site stood untouched by the darkness that slowly crept across FIGS.

Boomer was hiding behind one of the massive oak trees and Mac paused to yank him along.

"Come on!" she cried as the boy joined us. "For the trees!" Mac ordered.

We raced as fast as we could across the open lawn, knowing we were in plain sight. But it was the only way to get to the forest. Mac was ahead of me and Boomer behind. I tried to ignore the wails and cries coming from the others who were still attacking Soren.

We passed Dash's fallen form and saw that his skin had started to flake. Just like Doris's, his flesh was turning to dust. Would that happen to us all? I felt numb with grief.

I'll turn FIGS to dust. Soren's words chased me.

Another round of lightning struck the ground nearby and the shock knocked Boomer off his feet. I barely stayed upright and didn't notice Boomer was down until I put a few yards between us. I stopped to go back when a thick spiral of black fog latched around Boomer's ankle and yanked him away.

"Boomer!" I yelled. I went after him, but Mac yanked me back.

"We can't, Millie!" she cried. "We have to keep moving."

I struggled against her pull. "It's Boomer!"

Mac's face paled. A burst of dark fog shot toward us. The world slowed and I could hear my blood pounding in my ears. We couldn't move fast enough for it to miss us. We were finished.

As I braced myself to be hit, a blazing bright figure appeared between us and Soren. The shot of fog collided with the newcomer's chest, and she absorbed the blow. Our savior stumbled but did not fall.

"Dean Kyra!" I said.

"Run to the trees!" she commanded. Mac and I raced, Dean Kyra on our heels, and a few moments later we were under the cover of treetops.

I turned to the beautiful dean, shock still filling my chest. "Where . . ." I started, but I struggled to speak. I fell into her arms and she hugged me close. Mac did the same, pressing against my side, and for a split second I felt safe again.

Dean Kyra released us and we stepped back. I saw the scorch mark from the attack on her chest, deep and charred. An attack meant for me.

"Are you alright?" I asked.

"I'm fine, child. We must hurry," she said. "Come with me."

I sensed she was lying but followed her as she moved through the forest.

"What's happening?" Mac asked.

"Doris wrote in the *Book of History* and released Soren on FIGS," Dean Kyra said.

"Why would she do that?" I asked.

"Soren played on her insecurities and turned her into a Judas," Dean Kyra answered. She stopped and placed a hand on my shoulder. "You must not blame her for this."

I nodded and we started moving again. Dean Kyra was fast, and Mac and I were nearly running to keep up.

"What happened to the professors in the Children's Garden?" Mac asked. "And to Professor Gabriel? He was with Doris."

"Gone. They're all gone," Dean Kyra answered.

"But you can get them back," I said. "You can stop Soren, right?"

"I cannot," Dean Kyra said. "But he can be stopped."

"I don't understand," I said.

"You will," Dean Kyra said. "Come."

After a little while a small stone cave came into view. Dean Kyra turned to us.

"Listen to me, Millie. I cannot defeat Soren, but you can."

"What?" I said.

"You're the only one. It has always been you. The girl with the red medallion."

"I can't—"

"You can and you must, for the sake of all of FIGS." She grasped my medallion. "This will offer you protection against Soren. He cannot take it from you."

The charred place in the middle of her chest was turning to gray and beginning to flake. I stared at it. "Dean Kyra?"

She glanced down and then returned her eyes to mine. "I don't have much time." She released my medallion.

"No!" I begged. "Please don't leave me again."

"Oh, dear girl." She placed her hand on my cheek. "You don't need me. You have the Great Teacher, and he alone can show you how to finish this."

"I don't want to lose you," I said through tears. "I love you."

Her eyes misted as well. "I love you too, Millie Maven. But this is your path."

She looked to Mac, who was crying silently behind me. "And yours, Miss Spitzer. You'll need each other for what comes next. Your friendship is strong. Lean on that."

Then to Mac: "Protect her," Dean Kyra said.

Mac wrapped her arm through mine. "I will. I promise."

Dean Kyra motioned to the cave. "You'll find a pool inside. You must find Aggie. She'll tell you how to defeat Soren."

"Who's Aggie?" I asked.

"Someone in the world from which you came," Dean Kyra said. The flaking of her wound was spreading down her arms.

"You want us to leave FIGS?" Mac asked.

"It's the only way," Dean Kyra said. She dug something out of a pocket that was tucked inside her tunic. A slim strand of silver rope a yard long. She handed it to me.

"Tie yourselves together with this before you travel through the pool. It's very important you stay connected," Dean Kyra explained. "Do you understand?"

We nodded.

"Good. Go through the pool together and Aggie will be waiting. She'll explain everything else," Dean Kyra said. "You're the hope of FIGS, Millie."

She placed a kiss on the top of my head and then did the same to Mac. When she pulled back, a tear ran down her cheek. "I'm so proud of you both."

I wrapped my arms around the dean's waist, hugged her tightly, and tried not to weep. Dean Kyra held me for a moment and then softly pushed me back. "It's time, Miss Maven."

She placed a hand on my shoulder and her other

hand on Mac's. "Remember: As I have said from the beginning, this is a journey of the heart. And the lessons we teach you will change your worlds beyond FIGS. That has always been the purpose: understanding here at FIGS for understanding there."

I had questions, so many questions, but I knew our time was up. Dean Kyra gave our shoulders a squeeze, released us, and stepped away. Her skin was flaking off into the air.

"Go, and may the Great Teacher guide you," she said and then took off back toward the fight.

CHAPTER FIVE

Mac and I watched the dean until she was out of sight and then turned toward the cave. With Mac's arm looped through mine, we walked into the cave's opening. The stone arch couldn't have been more than eight feet high. Almost immediately we stumbled upon a brilliant-blue pool.

I looked down at the water, always amazed by the sight of it.

The way it moved.

The colors that swirled under the surface.

The way it called to me.

"I can't believe I never found this cave in all my exploring," Mac said.

"Maybe it only shows up when you need it," I suggested.

Mac nodded. Another mystery of FIGS to add to the list.

"You ready?" she asked.

"No," I said. I was filled with doubt and fear. What if it didn't work? What if we were separated? What if we couldn't get back? What if I wasn't strong enough to do what Dean Kyra believed I could?

"I'm afraid too," Mac said as if knowing the spirals of my mind. "But Dean Kyra believes in you. I believe in you. And I've got your back the whole way."

I smiled and felt a prick of relief. "Together."

"Together," she replied.

I placed the silver rope around our wrists and wrapped it three times. After securing it with a knot, Mac and I turned back to the pool.

"Stay close," I said.

"Here goes nothing," she said and we stepped into the water. Its pull tingled up my legs and body. We waded until the water was at our necks. With a final shared look, Mac and I plunged under the surface and swam for the light.

It surrounded us as we let the light pull us deeper. The water vanished, replaced by warm, comforting light. As it overtook my senses, I couldn't tell if Mac was still connected to my wrist. My world turned black.

I opened my eyes with a gasp and sat up. My first thought was Mac. The redhead lay beside me, damp and just waking. The silver cord still bound our wrists. Relieved, I smiled as Mac looked at me. The two of us worked together to stand.

We were in a much larger cave with a high rock ceiling and four torches stuck in the dirt around the water. Footsteps sounded and a person appeared from a tunnel.

The old woman had short, wild white hair. She wore black hiking boots and a homemade cloak and carried a burlap sack over her shoulder. The moment I saw her my memories came rushing back: Mother. Leaving the first time. Coming back while in the Shadowlands. Being locked in the basement. Escaping. Going back the second time. And every moment at FIGS since.

"Aggie," I said.

"Good. You made it through safely," Aggie said. She glanced at the rope still tied around our wrists. "It will be difficult to do this next part attached."

Mac set to untying us and within a few moments we were free.

"Keep the rope safe," Aggie said. "You'll need it for going back."

"Aggie," I said, pointing to Mac. "This is—"

"Mackenzie," Aggie said. "I know."

"My friends call me—" Mac started.

"Mac," Aggie finished. "I know."

"She knows many things," I said with a grin.

"True," Aggie continued. "Except how to talk to squirrels. They are the most stubborn, skittish creatures."

Mac leaned close. "Are you sure she isn't crazy?" she asked, her voice concerned.

I chuckled and shook my head. "Nope."

Mac looked wary for a moment and then smiled. "I prefer a little crazy." She looked around the cave. "Where are we?"

I opened my mouth to answer but Aggie cut me off. "Millie, we must be very careful what we reveal to Mackenzie about this place."

"Why?" I asked.

"Traveling through the pool is a delicate thing. *Her* story and the place *she* comes from cannot be compromised. In her journey *she* may be the girl with the red medallion, and we mustn't do anything to disrupt her learning."

"That doesn't make sense," Mac said. "Millie has the red medallion."

"Exactly," Aggie said. "So we understand one another."

Mac and I shared a confused look. "No," I said.

"It doesn't matter. Just promise me you won't tell Mackenzie anything more than I tell her now. It'll do more harm than good," the old woman said.

"I promise," I said. The last thing I wanted to do was cause Mac any harm.

"Good," Aggie said. "Let's begin." She turned and started back out the way she had come, yelling over her shoulder, "Follow me."

Mac and I followed as I rolled up the silver rope and tucked it into my pants pocket. We followed Aggie down a narrow tunnel and out into the sandy canyon. The sun had descended behind the mountains and I could see the moon making its nightly appearance.

"Whoa," Mac whispered, craning to look at the towering cliffs on either side. She'd slowed to admire.

"Keep up, girls," Aggie shouted.

I grabbed Mac's arm to tug her along. We caught up to Aggie at the edge of the forest. I knew where we were going and my heart started to race. This was the same path that took us back to my mother.

Why were we going back to my mother? If she discovered me, this time I'd never make it back to FIGS and all would be lost. Aggie must have noticed my hesitation.

"It's alright, Millie," Aggie said. "You'll see."

I followed her despite my fear, and a few minutes later we were at the edge of the woods. The mansion came into view, towering against the sky and surrounded by the tall iron fence.

My heart dropped into my gut as my mind replayed all the terror I had faced last time I was here. When I had escaped my mother's basement prison, I had been driven to save my friends, who'd been trapped in the Shadowlands. I'd been filled with courage and fueled by all I'd just learned in the golden field. I hadn't given a thought to what coming back might feel like or what consequences might be in store.

"What is this place?" Mac asked.

"This is where Millie grew up," Aggie said.

"Whoa," Mac said again. I could hear the wonder in her voice. "Are you like a princess or something?"

I shook my head. "Far from it." Then to Aggie. "What are we doing here? You know I can't be here."

"But this is where you must be," Aggie said.

"It isn't safe for me," I said.

"Isn't safe? I thought this was your home," Mac said.

"Home isn't always safe, Mac," I said.

She looked back to the looming mansion. "I wonder if the place I come from is safe." Mac turned to Aggie. "How come Millie can remember everything but I can't?"

"Because this is Millie's journey. She's the girl with the red medallion. This is her dream. Her world," Aggie said. "Yes?"

Mac opened her mouth to pry but I knew Aggie would only answer with more riddles. And FIGS was in danger. "Dean Kyra sent us to find you, Aggie," I said. "She said you could tell us how to defeat Soren."

"Yes. Dean Kyra. She's lovely," Aggie said.

"You know her?" I asked.

"I know this: The world of FIGS is designed to help you master your greatest gift, your heart. And I know that what's understood there is for the betterment of the world here."

"That's what Dean Kyra said, but I don't understand what that means," I said.

"It means, dear Millie, that when you deal with the darkness here, it will help you there. And when you deal with the darkness there, it will help you here. Simple, really."

I turned my gaze back to the only place I'd ever called home before FIGS.

"And here, my mother is the darkness," I said.

"Your mother," Mac said.

"Well, technically she is my aunt," I corrected.

"Then why do you call her mother?" Mac asked.

"My real mother died when I was little. My aunt,

Priscilla, is the only mother I have."

"So they say," Aggie said. She had said something like this before. As though the truth about my birth mother was different than I thought. I would have asked but Mac spoke first.

"Aunt Priscilla," Mac said. "Sounds like the name of an evil queen."

Mac didn't realize how spot-on she was. I felt her looking at me as I tried to stop dwelling on the dangers inside those walls.

"You're afraid of her," Mac observed.

"She's cruel and unkind and harsh and cold," I said. "The opposite of what I imagine a mother is supposed to be." I turned my attention back to Aggie, who was listening intently. "I don't know how to defeat my mother."

"You misunderstand, Millie," Aggie said. "You aren't going to defeat your mother."

She looked at me with a twinkle in her eyes. "You are going to save her."

"Save her? From what?" I asked.

"Her own fears and blindness. She's forgotten who she is, Millie, and you can remind her. And in doing so you will release your own grievance against her."

"I don't think I can," I said.

Aggie shrugged. "It's the only way to defeat Soren. As long as you hold fear in your heart, Soren will use it against you. He is the Father of Lies and he knows that fear will bring about more fear. As long as he can keep you enslaved to it, he will have power."

"But she is so cruel to me!"

"Yes, because she is so very blind and very afraid."

I huffed in disbelief. "Afraid of what?"

"The same things you are. That she isn't good enough. That no one loves her. That she's worth nothing."

"That's how she makes me feel!" I said, emotion gathering in my throat.

"Because that's how she feels. Fear only creates more fear, Millie. She believes those things about herself; therefore, she projects them onto you."

"But she's an adult and I'm just a kid."

Aggie smiled. "Thank goodness for that. Unless you become like a child, you cannot enter the kingdom. She needs you to remind her of the little girl inside who has never felt loved. Never felt worthy. You can do that, Millie. Love her even though she seems to be your enemy."

Aggie leaned down. "Like Doris seemed to be your enemy."

"That's different," I said. "The Great Teacher

loves Doris."

Aggie straightened. "Does the Great Teacher not love all?"

The second her words left her mouth I felt the warm sensation of the Great Teacher's love touch my heart. As I had many times before, I gasped in its presence. Did the Great Teacher love Aunt Priscilla as much as he loved me? Was I called to love her too?

As if a valve over my head had been twisted open, I felt the truth rush over me and knew the answer to my questions. "I'm not called to judge her but to love her," I whispered.

"By golly, I think she's got it," Aggie said.

"I feel the love of the Great Teacher for her," I said. Tears blurred my vision. "Do you really think I can help her see herself the way he does?"

Aggie smiled brightly. "I do, Millie Maven. Why do you think I took you to the pool on the night of your twelfth birthday? So you could get a superpower? No, dear girl, the reason was much more important than that."

Dean Kyra's words floated across my memory. *Remember: As I have said from the beginning, this is a journey of the heart. And the lessons we teach you will change your worlds beyond FIGS. That has always been the purpose.*

Could this be what she meant? If so, what did that mean for FIGS and my friends?

"I see you still have many questions," Aggie said, watching me closely.

"How does forgiving my mother help save FIGS?" I asked.

"Well, that part of the journey is for you to discover, but I know Priscilla Pruitt will play a crucial part."

"What do you mean?" Mac asked. She'd been so quiet, I had almost forgotten she was there.

"You understand the world of FIGS and this world are connected, yes?" Aggie said.

We nodded.

"What you learn there is for your benefit here and vice versa, yes?"

We nodded again.

"Good. It's time to step things up a level," Aggie said. "Your aunt needs a little push. I'm afraid she has become so blinded by her fear that it will take too long to convince her of the truth, and we all know we don't have that kind of time."

Aggie quickly moved to the iron fence, her burlap sack bouncing at her side, and started removing the pile of dry leaves that hid our route in and out of the property.

"But maybe if we got her to another place she would

be more receptive to love," Aggie said.

"Another place?" I said.

"Yes," Aggie said. "FIGS of course."

My mind exploded.

"Wait. You want us to take Millie's evil aunt back to FIGS?" Mac asked.

The statement was baffling. "That will never work. She'll never come with us!" I said.

"Not by choice," Aggie said.

What she was suggesting landed in my brain like a dropped anvil.

"You want to kidnap Millie's evil aunt," Mac said with a grin. "Awesomesauce."

Stunned, I looked at her. She shrugged.

"Yes, exactly, Mackenzie." I flipped my gaze to the old woman scooping leaves free from her hole. Aggie looked up at me. "Why are you looking at me as if I were mad?"

"Because this is an insane idea!" I said. "Soren is terrorizing FIGS! How will that help her get over her fear?"

"This isn't about Soren, my dear."

It wasn't? Nothing made sense. "We're just kids. We can't kidnap an adult."

"Let's not call it kidnapping if that makes you

uncomfortable," Aggie said. "Let's call it forcibly trans-ferring her somewhere else."

Mac leaned close and whispered, "Pretty sure that's the definition of kidnapping."

"You're not helping," I said. The wild woman finally finished clearing her hole. "Aggie, we really need to get back and save FIGS. You don't understand. Soren is completely destroying it. Can't I just forgive her from here? Can't you just tell me how to save everyone?"

"No, Millie, Priscilla must go with you. It's the only way," Aggie said.

"This can't be right," I said.

"Kyra sent you to me for a reason. You must trust me, girl! I've never led you astray, have I?"

She hadn't, but what she was suggesting . . .

"You promise it'll save FIGS?" I asked.

"It will save you, and you are FIGS," Aggie said. She stepped away from the hole. "But it will be dangerous."

"That's why I'm here," Mac said. "To protect her."

Aggie smiled at the redheaded girl. "And I'll go with you as well."

"You're coming?" I asked.

"Of course. You're just kids. You can't kidnap an adult alone."

Aggie winked and Mac giggled.

"Ready?" Aggie asked.

"Ready," Mac said.

I looked from one to the other, still uncertain.

Show them my love, Millie. Show them all.

I felt the Great Teacher near, and his words comforted me.

I nodded. "Ready."

CHAPTER SIX

Mac was the first one under the iron fence. I followed closely and Aggie squeezed through last, dragging her burlap sack. The air was cold, the sky dark, and the moon shone brightly. The night air nipped at my damp clothes and I shuddered.

Once under the fence we rushed behind the tall pines that shielded us from the house.

"Okay, what's the plan?" Mac asked.

"There are two very important pieces of information that make this the perfect evening for a kidnapping," Aggie said. "First, Mr. Pruitt left town yesterday morning for a weeklong business trip. So we won't have to worry about sneaking around him."

"He's your evil uncle?" Mac asked.

"Something like that," I answered.

"Second," Aggie continued, "Martha and Abby are away for Abby's weekly doctor appointment."

"Is she sick?" Mac asked.

I opened my mouth to answer and Aggie cut in.

"Millie, again I warn you not to overshare with Mackenzie. You do not want to face the consequences."

"I'll stop asking," Mac said.

"Thank you," Aggie said. "With Mr. Pruitt gone and the staff out of the house, we only have to worry about Roger. But I took care of him earlier."

"What does that mean?" I asked.

"I added some sleeping powder to his dinner tea. He should be fast asleep by now and wake up feeling completely refreshed tomorrow morning."

"Aggie!" I said.

"It's harmless," Aggie said. "And Roger is a good friend. I'll tell him everything myself once we've completed our task."

"If you slipped it into his tea before we came through the pool, then you knew we were coming," Mac said.

"Yeah, how did you know?" I asked.

"As I've said, I'm wise and know many things," Aggie said.

I was certain I'd heard Professor Gabriel say something similar. I didn't have time to dwell on it though, as Aggie was back to the plan.

"Tonight, Priscilla is our only concern," Aggie said.

"Three people to capture one," Mac said. "Should be a cinch."

"How do we get in?" I asked.

"Can you make your way back through the escape route you used from the basement?" Aggie asked.

"Wait," Mac said. "You had to escape from the basement?"

Aggie looked at the fiery girl and Mac offered an apologetic smile. "Sorry, no more questions."

Answering Aggie's question, I said, "I think so."

"Good. You and Mackenzie will sneak back into the basement, then come up and let me in through the kitchen side door."

"Why can't we all just go in the side door?" Mac asked.

"My mother is paranoid and keeps everything locked up pretty tight," I answered.

This made me think of the screws I'd put back in place on the air duct grate after escaping the basement. As if reading my mind, Aggie pulled a small screwdriver from her sack and held it out.

"This should help," she said.

I took it. "Thanks."

"What do we do once you're in?" Mac asked Aggie.

"Like you said, three to apprehend one," Aggie said.

"We don't know what we'll find in there," I said. "What if Mother gets away from us or something goes wrong?"

"Every adventure has its dangers," Aggie said. She placed her hand on my shoulder and held my eyes in the moonlight. "I know you're afraid, Millie. But I promise, this is the way to freedom. Remember when I took you to the pool and asked you if you wanted to change your life forever? All has led you here."

"And what if after all that I fail?" I asked.

"You won't, dear child. You won't."

The same confidence Dean Kyra, Professor Gabriel, and Rebecca had in me shone in Aggie's bright blue eyes. I just hoped I could find it in myself when it counted. I nodded and Aggie returned my gesture with a smile.

"Are you ready?" Aggie asked us. We nodded. "Good, I'll meet you at the kitchen."

"On three," Mac said, extending her hand into the middle of our small huddle. Aggie looked down at it.

"What's this?" she asked.

"You know, all hands in, then you count down and lift excitedly," Mac answered. "Like, yeah! Go, team! It's team-spirit stuff."

I watched, amused, as Aggie considered Mac's

explanation, smiled, and then playfully rubbed the top of Mac's head. "Go, team," the wild old woman said with a wink. Then she left us through the pines.

"I don't think she gets it," Mac said.

I chuckled and pulled Mac toward the house. "Follow me and keep low," I said.

She nodded and I led her out from the trees. Hunched over, I crossed the open ground, praying my mother wouldn't peer out a window and spot us. My fear rose at the thought and I pushed it away. I had to remain focused or this would never work.

We came alongside the mansion and kept close to the wall. I was careful to pass under the windows to avoid being spotted as we headed toward the rosebushes that lined the back of the house.

We slipped behind the bushes and dropped in front of the ventilation grate. I got to work on the screws while Mac kept glancing over the roses to make sure we hadn't been seen.

"Aggie is unusual," Mac whispered.

"Yeah," I replied.

"I like her. How'd you two meet?"

I gave her a side eye and she huffed. "I'm curious by nature. I don't know how to not ask."

When the last screw popped out, I carefully pulled

the grate away. I set it against the house and peered inside. The vent was dark. I didn't remember it being so dark. I didn't remember being so afraid either.

"Lead on," Mac said.

I took a deep breath and crawled into the duct, belly down, using my elbows to pull me forward. Mac entered and dinged the metal with something hard, maybe the toe of her shoe. The noise echoed.

"We have to be quiet," I whispered over my shoulder.

"Sorry."

I navigated to the best of my ability. What if we got to the basement and the grate had been replaced? It screwed closed from the inside. I wouldn't be able to get it loose. But Aggie had sent us this way. Maybe she had thought about that and somehow ensured it would still be open. Maybe she'd convinced Martha to help. Would Martha help me again?

Or maybe Mother left it open, hoping I would come back. Maybe she would be waiting for me and this was all a trap. Waves of fear rippled over my skin and wreaked havoc on my mind.

I took deep breaths and kept going. I had to get control of my mind. Rebecca had told me that in times of doubt and fear I should listen for the calming truth of the Great Teacher.

Don't be afraid. I am always with you.

I trusted his voice. I trusted Dean Kyra and Aggie. If this was my path, then I had to walk it, even if I was afraid.

I saw the square opening into the basement and felt a wave of relief. The grate was still detached. I wasn't sure why but I was grateful.

The white bucket was also still upended on the table. Nothing had been changed; it was exactly like I'd left it. I lowered myself through the opening and onto the bucket. Maybe Mother was hoping to find a clue as to where I had gone. I half expected to see yellow crime tape across the door.

I helped Mac exit the air duct and we both hopped down onto the concrete floor. The door was wide open and I glanced out to make sure the rest of the basement was clear.

"You were locked in here?" Mac asked.

I glanced back to see her scanning the bleak room. "I don't think I could forgive someone who locked me in a place like this." She looked at me with sorrow. "Do you really think you can love someone cruel enough to do this to you?"

On cue I felt the love of the Great Teacher pulse in my blood. I nodded. "Yeah, I do."

Mac gave her head a shake, a half grin pulling at the side of her mouth. "Maybe that's your gift," she said.

"Loving when most couldn't."

I'd never thought of it as a gift but maybe she was right.

"First Doris and now your evil aunt," Mac said.

"I love them because the Great Teacher did first."

Millie's smile grew. "You really are special, Millie Maven."

I was so happy she was with me.

"Now," she said with a smirk. "Let's go kidnap an adult."

She was having way too much fun, but I couldn't help smiling.

I motioned for her to follow. I left the room and quickly crossed the basement to the stairs. One at a time, with careful steps, we climbed to the door. I placed my hand on the knob, turned it slowly, and pushed it open just enough to look out.

The wide hallway on the first floor was empty. It was shadowed with night and still as the dead. I pushed the door farther open and crept out. Mac followed and then, to cover my tracks, I carefully clicked the door shut.

I placed a finger over my lips to ensure Mac knew we absolutely could not speak. With a nod of confirmation from her, I moved down the hall. The kitchen was at the back of the house but on the other side of the grand staircase. There was a small walkway that crossed behind the stairs, and I was grateful we didn't have to pass by the front.

Near the kitchen entrance, I checked for Mother and then pulled back behind the cover of the wall. "Okay," I whispered. "You first. It's the first door on the right."

"We should go together," Mac replied.

"It might make too much noise," I said. "It's safer to go one at a time. Don't worry, I'm right behind you."

Mac hesitated before nodding. I glanced out to confirm it was still clear and then motioned for her to go. Mac quickly crept out into the hallway, up the middle, and then pushed through the kitchen door

I was about to follow when the light in the hallway flicked on and filled the area with bright light. I fell back behind my cover and held my breath. My heart rammed against my ribs.

"Hello?" a familiar female voice called. "Who's there?"

Mother.

"I've already called the police! They'll be here any minute." I could hear the quiver in her voice and knew her words were a lie. Mother hated the police. She'd rather be burglarized.

I tried to form a strategy. I could go back the way I'd

come, but I'd never make it into the basement without her hearing, and if I tried going around the stairs she'd see me for sure.

I was stuck.

Panic tumbled in my gut as I searched for any way out. But there wasn't one. I thought about Mac huddled behind the kitchen door. I wouldn't put it past her to spring out and try to protect me. I couldn't let that happen. Aggie had warned against Mac learning too much. I couldn't risk what would happen if my mother caught her.

There was only one thing to do. I swallowed and stepped out from my hiding spot into the light. Shock flashed across Mother's face, then disbelief, followed by anger.

"Millie," she growled.

"Hello, Mother." I tried to keep my tone strong. Inside I was trembling like a leaf. We stood there for a long moment before she broke the stillness and strode toward me with angry steps.

I needed to get her away from the kitchen. I raced for the other side of the house.

"Millie Maven, you come back here right now!" Mother yelled.

I exited the passageway, Mother's clicking heels

close behind. I ran past the basement door and toward the first-floor library.

"Millie!" Mother screamed.

I rounded the front of the stairs and saw Mac poke her head out of the kitchen door. Catching her attention, I motioned for her to go back. She looked unwilling and I frantically mouthed, *Get back*, praying my friend would heed my words.

Mac ducked back into the kitchen as my mother came into view.

"How dare you run from me!" she yelled.

"I'm sorry." I raised my hands in surrender. "Please listen to me."

She stopped five feet away, face red, eyes filled with anger. "Listen to you!"

"Let me explain—"

"Yes, explain, Millie. Explain why twice in a week you have betrayed me, broken every rule imaginable, and done who knows what with that crazy witch who lives in the woods!"

"Mother, please," I begged. "It's so much more than that. So much more than you could imagine!"

Fear sparked amid her anger. "What does that mean? What have you been doing? You wretched, ungrateful creature!"

The strength I'd gathered was melting away. Fire was spilling from her eyes and my body started to quake as she inched closer, daring me to cross her again. My mind froze. My heart raced. I felt like a rabbit caught in a trap. I should have known better than to come back.

"What?" she spat. "Tell me, you wicked child!"

"I . . . I . . ." Fear blurred my vision and bogged down my brain. I couldn't see through it.

"I, I, I," she mocked in a squeaky voice. "You are nothing. I risked everything for you. I brought you into my home and tried to make you better, but you are worthless!"

She crossed to me in two long strides and grabbed my arm. I wanted to crumple at her feet, melt into the floor, hide from the heaps of shame that fell from her mouth.

Years of pain and terror rose in me and for a moment all I felt was fear.

But I was not the same girl I'd been, and the small voice of truth came to me quickly. *Fear only creates more fear. Offer love to the things you fear. For love casts out fear.*

Dean Kyra's words emerged from the small reaches of my heart, and with them came a call to remember who I was. Life was a cycle of remembering and forgetting. My fear had made me forget the power of the Great Teacher: his love, which was strong enough to help me love those I feared most.

I released my fear and chose to stand in love.

"Tell me where you have been!" Mother yelled. She still squeezed my arm, but I wasn't resisting her or flinching under her wrath. In the Shadowlands I'd learned to love my enemies. To see them as me. I had only momentarily forgotten.

I smiled, and for a second my mother cowered.

"I can do more than tell you," I said. "I can show you."

My reply derailed her anger and she frowned. "What do you mean?"

"I've been to an incredible place filled with wonder and beauty. You'd love it, Mother."

Her grasp eased and a dozen emotions crossed her face. She wasn't sure how to react to me.

"I've been learning things there about life and love. Things that have set me free from my fears."

"What nonsense are you spouting?" Mother hissed.

"It's not nonsense," I said as she released my arm completely. "It's truth. Beyond what our eyes can see. I'll show you." I extended my hand and she backed away as if it were diseased.

Her eyes flickered from my hand to my face a few

times. For a moment I thought maybe Aggie had been wrong about her. Maybe she would just come with us.

Then darkness washed across her expression and the spark of hope died in my chest. She recaptured my arm and yanked me close to her face.

"You listen to me, you little brat." Her spit landing against my cheek. "You're going to tell me everything if I have to beat it out of you. Then you and I are going somewhere far away where no one will ever be able to find you."

My fear surged. "Away?"

"Enough out of—" she started, but a sharp crack cut her off. For a moment her eyes widened, then she released my arm and slumped to the floor.

Aggie stood behind her, frying pan in hand, raised near her head.

Wide-eyed, Mac came up beside her.

They'd just hit my mother with a frying pan.

Chapter Seven

"You knocked her out," I said.

"I must be stronger than I thought," Aggie said, lowering her arms. She saw the distress on my face and winked at me. "Don't worry. She'll have a goose egg, nothing more."

Mac came to my side. "Are you okay?"

"I'm fine," I answered.

"We shouldn't have split up," Mac said. "You could've been in real trouble."

I saw the concern in Mac's eyes. Dean Kyra had asked her to protect me, and I guessed she felt like she had almost failed.

"If you hadn't gotten Aggie I would be, so thanks," I said.

Her tension eased. "From now on we stay together."

"Okay."

Aggie dropped down next to my fallen mother and turned the woman onto her side. Aggie set her burlap sack on the ground, reached inside, and pulled out a spool of rope.

"Be careful," I said.

Aggie nodded. "Of course, dear, just like tying up a prize hog." She carefully bound my mother's wrists and ankles together. Then she reached back into her sack and pulled out a bandana, which she tied around Mother's mouth.

"Is that necessary?" I asked.

"Would you like her to come to in the middle of the woods and alert the wolves?" Aggie asked casually.

Mac and I exchanged a fearful look.

"Why does it always have to be wolves?" Mac said under her breath.

"Help me," Aggie called as she prepared to load my mother onto her shoulders. Mac and I each lifted one side as Aggie got her weight under the woman and pressed up to standing.

"You really are stronger than you look," Mac said.

Aggie headed for the kitchen, my mother laid across her shoulders. "Grab my things," she said.

We did, then followed Aggie through the kitchen and out into the backyard. We traveled across the yard, back to the pines, and then one by one under the fence. It took us some doing to push and pull my mother through. In the process we ripped the sleeve of her silk blouse.

She wouldn't be happy about that. Familiar cycles of fear started to run in my chest again. But I was getting better at remembering the truth, so the fear didn't feel overwhelming.

Once under the fence we helped Aggie heft my mother and headed into the woods. By the time we entered the sandy canyon, a light snow had started to fall. It stuck to the sand as we crossed toward the cave.

Aggie had to turn sideways to navigate Mother down the narrow path that led to the pool. When I saw the water, the chill in my bones warmed. I couldn't believe we were actually doing this.

Aggie carefully set my mother down next to the pool and reached out for her burlap sack, which Mac handed to her.

"We must move quickly," Aggie said. "FIGS needs you both."

She dug into her sack and pulled out a small vial of red liquid. It looked like strawberry Kool-Aid. She pulled the bandana off Mother's mouth.

The plump woman started to twitch and moan.

Aggie parted the woman's lips and poured a few drops from the vial onto her tongue. Mother swallowed instinctively and her eyes fluttered open.

Her eyes darted to me, to Mac, to Aggie, to the ropes around her ankles and wrists. She opened her mouth to scream and Aggie cupped her palm over her lips.

"Scream and I'll bonk you again," Aggie said.

I knelt beside them. "It's alright, Mother," I said. "You'll see."

She looked between Aggie and me, terrified. Aggie slowly removed her hand and Mother just sat there, trembling like a scared cat.

Aggie handed Mac the vial. "You both need to drink this," she said. "It will allow you to remember the things you experienced here once you go back."

Mac took a swallow and handed it to me so I could do the same.

"You must be united," Aggie said. "Your aunt with you. You still have the silver rope, Millie."

I pulled it from my pocket and handed it over. Aggie undid the knot at my mother's ankles and we all stood.

"Don't even think about running," Aggie said. "I grew up in these woods and I have furry friends with teeth."

"Let me go," Mother said. "I won't say anything to anyone. Millie, darling."

I laid my hand on her forearm. I had never seen the woman in such a state and it broke my heart. "I promise you, everything will be okay."

"You must go now," Aggie said. She began to tie us together with the silver rope and I tried to offer my mother courage. Once we were through the pool, she would see.

"What do we do once we're back?" I asked. "How do we defeat Soren?"

After yanking the knots tight, Aggie moved her hand to my cheek and smiled. "You'll know. The Great Teacher will lead you."

"Can't you come with us?" Mac asked.

Aggie chuckled. "No, dear Mackenzie. My place is here." She ruffled Mac's red hair again. "Now go."

Dread filled me. Taking my mother back to FIGS would be dangerous for her. I glanced back at Aggie. Her face softened and she reached for my hand.

"Come here, child." She pulled me away from my mother and Mac. Her tone was low and kind. "I can see you're worried."

"Won't it be dangerous to take my mother to FIGS with everything happening there?"

"It's the only way," Aggie said. "But let me ease your mind. Your aunt is neither a child nor part of the FIGS program. Soren can't do anything to her."

Relief filled me.

"Except kill her of course," Aggie said.

"What?" My relief vanished.

"Trust me. You'll see," Aggie said.

Before I could respond, she said, "And your red medallion gives you extra protection from the darkness." Dean Kyra had told me the same thing. "It cannot be taken from you. And only you can offer it up."

"What does that mean?" I asked. Why would I offer it up?

She placed a hand on my cheek and grinned, ignoring my question. "You were made for this, dear Millie. Always listen to the voice of the Great Teacher and you will see."

I nodded, still afraid, but I had to trust her.

We returned to my mother and Mac and then went to the water's edge, my quivering mother in tow.

"I don't understand what's happening," she said.

"We're going swimming," Mac said with a smirk.

My mother's face paled and she started shaking her head. She inched back from the pool.

"You don't have time for this." Aggie gave my mother

a nudge. "She will see all once you're there. Swim down and keep her close."

We waded into the water, deeper and deeper, Mother so shocked that she stopped fighting.

"Hold your breath, Mother," I said and a moment later we were all beneath the surface. I pulled Mother along as I swam, Mac assisting. Mother resisted for only a moment and then saw the bright light that beckoned us.

The process happened the same as before. Captured by the light, we swam toward it until we each lost consciousness. We all woke beside a different pool in a different place.

I sat up, still tethered to Mac and my mother, who were waking at the same time. I quickly untied us and helped my mother stand. She rubbed the spot at the back of her head where Aggie had hit her and looked around the small cave. She glanced down at her clothes, realizing they were damp, then looked at me with fearful eyes.

"Where . . . how . . ."

"It's okay." I grabbed her hand. "Come, I'll show you."

I pulled the stunned woman out of the cave to show her the world I had come to love dearly. But I nearly collapsed at what I saw. Charred trees, leafless and bare, were the only proof that a beautiful dense forest had thrived here.

Ash and dust covered the ground, making the surface a pervasive gray. Black clouds filled the sky and stole most of the sun's light and heat.

Mac stumbled out after me and gasped. "Oh my gosh," she whispered.

My soul ached. The world of FIGS was destroyed.

"The school," I said.

I yanked my mother along and started running.

"Millie, wait," Mac called. But I ignored her. Surely the school was still standing. Mother stumbled behind me as I ran.

"Millie!" Mac called again. "Slow down."

I couldn't. I raced through the dead forest and saw the truth before I was ready. My knees and my heart sank at the same time. My mother collapsed beside me. It couldn't be! Mac soon caught up to us.

"No," she groaned.

Only a stone foundation, a damaged wall, and a few pillars stood where the school had been. Everything else was gone. The gravel path that led to the entrance had turned to dust. Blackened skeletons were all that remained of the once-grand oak trees.

"He did it," I whispered. "Soren destroyed FIGS."

"This can't be right," Mac said. "We brought your aunt here. We're supposed to be able to save them."

"We're too late," I said. "There's nothing left to save."

"No! We did what we were told. Dean Kyra said—"

"Dean Kyra was wrong, Mac! And she isn't here to help. No one is here!"

Tears filled my eyes as Mac searched for words to help. But there weren't any.

"We failed," I said.

Mac shook her head and laid her hand on my shoulder. "No, Millie, there must be a way."

"Mac—"

"I know. It looks bleak, but we can't give up."

I shook my head as tears slipped down my cheek.

"Look at me, Millie," Mac said.

I did.

"You were chosen by the Great Teacher. He gave you the red medallion. You found the golden vial when the rest of us got lost in darkness. You went back to the place that imprisoned you and offered love to your evil aunt, in spite of all she's done to you."

I felt Mother's eyes on me as Mac continued.

"I know you don't always believe in yourself, but I'm telling you, Millie Maven, you're special and I believe in you. You do things no one else can. This isn't over."

I sighed and nodded. Maybe she was right. There had to be a way. Dean Kyra wouldn't have sent us to Aggie, and Aggie wouldn't have sent us back if there wasn't a way.

"Together," Mac said.

"Together," I replied.

"This can't be real," my mother whispered.

I turned to speak to her and saw a black coil of fog running along the ashy ground toward us.

"Run!" I yelled. I grabbed Mother's hand and yanked her up. We dashed away from our attacker and into the woods. Our shoes kicked up dust that stuck to our wet clothes and filled our lungs. It was everywhere.

Mac slid to a stop and I nearly tumbled into her. She inched backward and I saw another coil coming toward us. We had to get out of the forest. Mac led as we raced for an escape. After bursting out onto FIGS's front lawn, we ran along the dead tree line toward the dim sun.

More black tendrils pursued us from all angles, slithering along the ground like hunting serpents. The clouds rumbled and began to shift. A long cylinder of swirling darkness became a small tornado and touched down on the ground a hundred yards away.

The dead branches bent to the storm's will. Our clothes flapped in the violent wind and I could feel my body being pulled toward the twister. It was moving toward us, winds so strong it was hard to move.

"We need to find cover!" The storm nearly drowned out Mac's voice. I felt like I was running through quick-sand, every step labored as the tornado closed in. Mac led us back into the woods, searching for shelter.

"The cave!" I cried.

The twister yanked trees from their roots and devoured them in its swirling funnel.

Mother was holding my hand so tightly my fingers had gone numb. She yanked my arm back and I tumbled to the ground. Mother had fallen, her kitten heels caught on something beneath the ash. She released my hand and struggled to free her foot.

I tried to help as the tornado closed in. But Mac grabbed me back just as Mother's foot popped loose from her shoe.

"We can't stop!" Mac yelled.

Mother stood and started racing after us again when a thick tendril shot from the approaching twister. It wrapped around Mother's chest like a lasso and tugged her backward.

It happened so quickly.

She screamed and fell to the ground, thrashing against the fog's hold.

"Mother!" I cried.

"No, Millie!" Mac yelled as she held me tight and pulled me away. "We can't stop!"

My mind was numb as I watched the storm take my mother, terrified screams spilling from her throat. I tugged against Mac, but she was stronger.

"This way!" Mac shouted.

"We can't leave—"

"If we don't go, it will get us too! Now, Millie!"

I fought everything in me that wanted to go after my mother. I saw where Mac was headed, toward a ravine that cut into the earth. If we could drop down over the edge, maybe we could find cover from the storm.

Wind whipped at us. The edge was near and Mac pulled me around in front of her and pushed me toward it. For the first time I saw how steep it was.

"Take my arm," Mac said. "I'll help you down."

I didn't have time to think, only follow her commands. I dropped to my knees and scooched backward over the edge, my hand tightly grasped around Mac's forearm. Still secure on the ravine's high ledge, I glanced down. The ground was more than ten feet down. I was going to have to drop and pray I could absorb the landing.

"Mac," I said, afraid this wasn't going to work.

Before she could answer, her face paled and her eyes widened. She glanced back at her ankle. A tendril of darkness had wrapped around her leg.

Mac frantically tried to kick it off with her free foot, but the more she struggled the larger it grew. It dragged her away from the edge, pulling me with her.

"Mac! No!" Not Mac. I couldn't do this without her.

Suddenly she stopped fighting. The fog slowly inched up her leg. As though she'd remembered something, recognition lit her eyes.

"Let go, Millie," she said.

"No!" I cried. "I won't."

The dark fog yanked harder. The forest floor scraped my stomach raw. Ash filled my mouth and caused my eyes to water.

"It's okay," Mac said. "You have to let go!"

"No, I can't do this alone!"

"I have to protect you," Mac said. "You're the girl with the red medallion."

I shook my head. I couldn't do what she was asking.

One more time the fog yanked on us. The tendril of darkness reached up to Mac's waist, ensuring an unbreakable hold on her. The wind still battered us and ash rained from the sky.

"Let go, Millie," Mac said again. In the midst of

chaos her voice was calm. "Don't be afraid. You are never alone."

Tears stung my eyes and I knew I had to release her. Even as she reminded me of the powerful truth, I had to let her go. She smiled and I unlatched my fingers from her arm.

The fog monster didn't waste a second. It yanked Mac away from me, back across the forest floor and up into the wind tunnel. In half a second Mac was gone. The tornado died away, the howling wind calmed, and the ashy, dead land stilled.

I didn't move. I laid there facedown in the dust with only the sounds of my pounding heart and ragged breath to keep me company. Everything else was gone. Dead. Destroyed.

I was all that remained.

CHAPTER EIGHT

I pushed myself off the ground, my legs shaking as I stood. I expected the darkness to return any moment and snuff me out. But it didn't, which was worse, because it might have been easier to be eaten by Soren than to be the only person left.

I didn't understand. I'd done what Dean Kyra asked. I'd gone to Paradise, I'd followed Aggie's instructions, and I'd brought my mother back to FIGS because I believed all those who said I could save everyone.

Maybe I did something wrong.

Was all lost?

A soft breeze nipped at the back of my neck and I turned, half expecting to see the fog. Instead I saw two large, fat, burned trees standing close together and reaching into the sky. I would have thought nothing of them, but the soft breeze came again, seeming to pass through the small space between the trunks. Had the trees been there before?

Only the dead forest lay beyond them, and the breeze seemed to come from the gap. I stepped toward the trees carefully. The closer I got, the stronger the sense I had that something was different with these trees.

I reached them and placed my hand on the bark of one. It felt rough and solid and was flaky with ash. The light wind ruffled my hair. On a hunch, I stepped through the space.

The world around me shifted. The dead forest changed to a beautiful living garden. One I had seen before. One I would never forget.

This was the Great Teacher's garden, where I had first met Rebecca, filled with brilliant and exotic flowers, trees, birds, and bushes. The lush garden went on as far as I could see, eclipsing all signs of Soren's wasteland. It was warm and filled with light. A stunning rainbow arced above me, and white fluffy clouds dotted the blue sky.

Behind me, where the dark trees should have been, was a wall of thick ivy. Under my feet, the stone path Professor Gabriel had first led me down. The thought of the wise, sweet old man made me mournful.

The path would lead to the fountain. I started

walking. A few moments later I saw it, the shimmering water cascading down over the stone terraces. The blue-green liquid was identical to the water in the pools. It was the same water I'd sipped on my first visit to the garden. This water had allowed me to hear the Great Teacher's voice.

Could it help me now?

"You don't need the water now, my sweet girl," her warm voice said.

Rebecca appeared from behind a tall rosebush. She wore her gardening gloves and boots.

"You already allowed the Great Teacher into your heart," Rebecca said. "He is always with you."

"Soren destroyed everything," I said. "He took everyone." I could feel my tears brewing and my sorrow threatening to snuff out my words. "He's too powerful. I don't know how to fight him. I'm just a girl."

"Yes, the girl with the red medallion," Rebecca said. She came to me, her smile warm. "Don't be discouraged, Millie Maven. Every moment has led you here so you can understand the power the red medallion symbolizes."

I lifted the medallion from my shirt. The red circle gleamed in the light of the sun. "How?" I asked in a whisper.

"You were chosen by the Great Teacher to follow

his path," she said. "To first know you are wholly loved, then to see his love for others, and now to love even your worst enemy. To surrender all to his love, a love that casts out all fear. As the Great Teacher has done, he calls you to do as well."

She retrieved a small white leather book from behind her back and held it out to me. I gasped and accepted it.

"The Great Teacher's journal, the one Dean Kyra gave me."

"When the student is ready, the teacher appears," Rebecca said. She placed a soft hand on my shoulder and leaned down to kiss the top of my head. Then she stepped back. "You are ready, Millie Maven."

I looked down at the journal in my hands and touched the engraving of the sword on its cover. The sword of truth. I exhaled, unsure Rebecca was right. When I looked up to tell her so, she was gone, nowhere to be seen.

I walked to the fountain and sat on its stone edge. Ankles crossed, journal on my lap, I cracked open the cover and turned to the first page. It was blank, as it had been every other time I had looked. I nearly shut the book.

But the page started to shimmer and words began

to appear, one at a time, in lines across the page. What was once blank filled with sentences. I stared, stunned. The warm breeze swirled around me, and I knew the presence of the Great Teacher was with me as I read the text.

Daughter, let me tell you the ways I love you.

I love you more than the light of a million stars.

I call you perfect, whole, washed clean in my death and life. Don't be afraid. I am with you always.

These were words I had heard him say before, but now they were written in ink, a tangible reminder of his promises and love. This was the Great Teacher's journal of truth.

I am in all. All are created in my image.

As you do unto others you do unto me.

Bless those who come against you, for they have only forgotten they are perfectly loved.

Silent tears ran down my cheeks as the love of the Great Teacher filled my heart and soul. I turned the page. Again, words began to appear.

There is no fear in love, for love casts out fear.

You have not been given a spirit of fear, daughter, but of power and love. When you stand with me, who can stand against you? Even death has no sting.

I turned the page again and still more invisible

words made themselves known.

I tell you, daughter, unless a seed falls to the ground and dies, it remains only a seed. But in death it bears the fruit of new life.

This is my commandment, that there is no greater love than to lay down one's life for a friend.

I read these pages over and over, trying to sear the words into my brain and onto my heart. Tears dropped off my chin and marked the pages of the journal. None of it felt new to my heart. The truths summarized all the lessons I'd been learning since Aggie had led me to the pool the night of my birthday and I'd discovered FIGS.

Lessons from Dean Kyra, Aggie, Rebecca, Professor Gabriel, and the rest. All were designed by the Great Teacher to show me the way. I could feel his truth in my bloodstream.

Sitting there in the garden, I began to understand the fullness of my path. The Great Teacher had called me, chosen me, and given me the red medallion. He'd shown me the power of his love for me and then had let me feel it for others, even my greatest enemy.

Mother.

In every trouble I'd encountered, the message had always been the same: Love is greater than any fear.

More than that, in perfect love there is *no* fear. But the choice to love had to be mine. Love or fear. I could not do both at the same time.

My fears washed over me and I heard them like whispers around my head.

I was afraid of not being enough. I was afraid of being worthless.

Afraid of being alone. Afraid of losing all those I loved.

Afraid of failing.

Afraid of Soren.

The Great Teacher's voice came to me on the breeze. *Don't be afraid, for I am always with you. I have already overcome all darkness. All I call you to do, daughter, is love. Let go of your fears. Be filled with my love.*

I closed the journal and held it tightly to my chest. Tears, warm on my cheeks, continued to fall off my chin as my fears washed away.

Do not resist when evil comes against you, rather love as I have loved. Only in surrender will you know the fullness of my love. A love without fear. Follow me, daughter. I named and knew you before the beginning of time. Follow me in love.

Could I follow the path of the Great Teacher? Could I stand in the presence of darkness and not be afraid?

Even of dying? Was the love of the Great Teacher that powerful?

I knew it was. I could feel it in my bones, and the longer I sat there on the edge of the stone fountain, the stronger my certainty became. I knew the path ahead of me was clear. The choice was clear: I would stand in love.

I wasn't sure how much longer I sat there, eyes closed, letting the presence of the Great Teacher fill me. But when I opened my eyes and saw the garden was no longer there, I wasn't afraid.

The journal I had held against my chest vanished too. This surprised me. Immediately the red medallion began to vibrate hot on my skin. I jerked it out and felt its power in my fingers. The simple crown was still engraved on the medallion's front. I slowly turned it over and saw that a sword—the same sword engraved on the leather journal's cover—was etched into my medallion, piercing through the heart engraved there.

The sword of truth was with me, over my heart!

I had the protection of the red medallion, which couldn't be taken from me, and the sword of truth.

Slipping my medallion under my shirt, I looked through the trees and knew what I had to do. My feet didn't hesitate. My path was clear, set before me by the Great Teacher. Yes, it was narrow, but it had been chosen for me. I walked through the trees toward my destination, the power of love coursing through me.

It was time to face Soren.

And I was ready.

CHAPTER NINE

My feet knew where to go. They were being guided by my heart, and my heart was being led by the Great Teacher out of the dead forest, across the front lawn of FIGS, and toward the small amphitheater where the day had started. The first place Soren had destroyed.

The air was still and thick with dust. The love of the Great Teacher made my footsteps light and confident as I approached. I heard the cries of someone familiar and I paused, experiencing a spike of fear, a moment of hesitation. But as quickly as the fear came, the power of love soothed it.

Perfect love beyond my fears. This is where I had to stand.

I moved more quickly and the cries of anguish grew louder. The amphitheater's arched entryway barely stood, most of it reduced to ash. I stepped through and took in the dire scene.

The sky was darker here than anywhere else. The beauty of the plant growth was gone, incinerated. The stone seating had crumbled as though a plague of insects had devoured it. The stone statues remained, though a couple had been knocked to the ground. The thick bushes and tall trees that surrounded the amphitheater's small stage were nothing but dead limbs. Half the stone stage had eroded.

A stone wall stood behind the stage. I hadn't seen it before because it had been blocked by the trees, now withered. Ten feet off the ground a person hung on the wall, pinned in place by tendrils of thick fog. One was wrapped around her rib cage and another around her throat.

My mother, her face pale. Lines of mascara and eyeshadow smeared her cheeks. Her mouth hung open in a terrified scream.

The dark tendrils of fog snaked across the ground like veins. A large tunnel of darkness, black as night, hovered over what remained of the stage. The fog beast. Soren. It pulsed with fear because it was fear personified.

The sight of my mother held by the darkness sparked another hesitation in my chest. Again the love of the Great Teacher softly ushered me back to love. *Yes*, I thought. *Love over fear.*

The fog slowly turned toward me as if sensing my presence. The beast transformed from fog to a man. I knew the face, though dark tendrils still snaked from his form.

Soren. His heavy cloak hung to the ground. The hood cast most of his white skin in shadow. But his red eyes were clear.

"I knew you would come," he said. "Your delusional belief in love is too strong for you to resist."

"Love casts out fear," I said.

"Don't you feel afraid?" Soren asked.

I wanted to lie and say I didn't, but I could sense from the way he was looking at me that he already knew. It had been easier to stand in love when I hadn't been face to face with evil. I searched for the strength of love beyond fear but could still feel the tremble of panic in my fingers.

"I can feel your fear," Soren said. "Of course you're afraid. You're just a girl with no weapons or skills or gifts. How could you possibly stand against me?"

Soren held out his hands proudly. "I am the Father of Fear. Destroyer of worlds. I have power beyond your wildest imagination. What are you?"

I opened my mouth to speak but Soren cut me off.

"I know what you are. Scared, lonely, worthless. You're trying to convince yourself you're something more, but the truth is there, deep and certain. I know you feel it. I've been trying to help you see clearly from the beginning."

"You're a liar," I said.

"No, the Great Teacher is the one who has lied to you. From the start he's been filling your mind with ideas about who you are. That's what he does. He claims to have overcome darkness, yet where is he now? Where is his power?"

Soren inched toward me. Behind him on the wall, my mother wept.

"I destroyed him. I exposed his false promises and showed the truth to the ones he tricked. I opened their eyes to see with the wisdom of the world. They killed the Great Teacher because they finally saw who they really were: miserable, fearful, worthless people."

The voice of the Great Teacher filled my mind. *Do not resist when evil comes against you; rather, love as I have loved. Only in surrender will you see the fullness of my love.*

Unless a seed dies it cannot bear fruit. I made a way for love, even in death.

His words filled me with understanding.

"Don't you see, Millie Maven?" Soren said. "This is the only way. My way."

"I do see," I said. "I see that even in death the Great Teacher shows the power of love. A love that casts out fear. A love beyond fear."

Soren's eyes closed to slits. "There is nothing beyond fear and death, you foolish girl."

"But the Great Teacher isn't dead," I said. I could feel my skin tingling with power and certainty. "He's alive and with me now. I feel his love, stronger than my fear. You didn't destroy him. You can't."

Soren flinched and I took a step forward. "The only power you have is to blind us to who we really are: children of the Great Teacher."

Heat like fire rose up my back and I experienced the presence of the Great Teacher as I continued. "He calls me daughter. He says I am chosen. He offers his perfect love without condition." I yanked the medallion from my shirt. It was warm in my palm and seemed to glow.

"He gave me his red medallion." I looked up at Soren, whose face was twisted in anger. "And you've been trying to convince me I was worthless from the moment we met."

Something new dawned in my mind and I took another step forward. "Because you know that if I stand in love, you have no power over me."

"No power?" Soren raised his hands and whipped the wind into violence. The clouds darkened and thunder crashed against the sky. The tendrils of fog coming from his form grew and rose.

I raised my hands against the vicious winds. Their blows almost knocked me off my feet.

"I have already destroyed and taken everything from you, Millie Maven. Your home, your friends, all those you love!" Soren cast his eyes back to my mother, whose body quivered with fear. "And now you will watch as I snuff out the final piece."

He rolled his fingers into a fist and the tendril around my mother's throat tightened. She started choking, her pinned arms unable to offer any defense.

"Stop," I cried. The sight of it caused me to panic. This couldn't be happening. I had to stop it!

Don't be afraid, for I am always with you. I have already overcome all darkness.

"But he'll kill her," I whispered, trying to listen through the return of my fears. Aggie had said Soren could kill her if he wanted.

You have not been given a spirit of fear, daughter, but of power and love. When you stand with me, then who can stand against you? Even death has no sting.

Only in surrender will you see the fullness of my love. A love without fear. Follow me, daughter, the one I named and knew before the beginning of time. Follow me in love.

My fear subsided even as I watched my mother struggle in Soren's grasp, even as I heard my mind screaming at me to fight, to resist. Even as the wind whipped around me and the sky continued to storm, my fears vanished.

The red medallion tingled in my hand and I glanced down to see the humble crown etched into its surface. *Surrender*, I thought. *I must let go of my fear. Even the fear of death, because the Great Teacher has already overcome it.* Again Aggie's words returned to me: *It cannot be taken from you. And only you can offer it up.* I could sacrifice it, and I knew what I had to do.

I yanked the red medallion off my neck and held it out high in front of me. "I will take her place!" I called above the swirling storm.

The wind halted and the thunder calmed. Soren turned back to me, his eyes ablaze with hate.

"I will take her place," I said again, the medallion dangling from my grasp. "Leave her. You can have me." I was giving up the red medallion's protection, but I would follow the Great Teacher. And I wasn't afraid.

"After all she has done to you?" Soren hissed.

Forgive them, for they know not what they do. This new phrase drifted through my mind and filled me with peace.

I locked eyes with my mother. They were red and filled with horror. Her face was filled with pain. I offered her a soft smile and felt tears gather in my bottom lids.

"I forgive you," I said to the woman.

Shock pulsed across her expression, then she crumpled into self-pity.

To Soren I said, "Take me instead."

A tendril snaked out toward me, wrapped around the red medallion, and yanked it from my grasp. The tendril pulled the medallion toward Soren and he snatched it from the air. He held it in his palm, turning it over, seemingly fascinated. For a long second the world stilled. Then Soren dropped the medallion to the ground and crushed it against the stone with the heel of his boot.

The brilliant red color drained from the metal and it returned to its original bronze state. My heart ached. Yet something inside me calmed, as if I still had a lesson to learn.

"Such a foolish mistake," Soren hissed. He yanked

my mother's weeping body off the wall and tossed her aside. She landed with a thud and her cries intensified. I rushed to offer comfort, but a black tendril wrapped around my waist and hoisted me off the ground.

It jerked me through the air, my feet dangling, and drew me to a sharp stop in front of Soren. I could feel the anger pulsing from his eyes.

"So quick to offer yourself in the name of love," Soren said. The thick coil that held me slammed me against the wall where my mother had been, secured me tightly, and expanded until I was wrapped in darkness from my chest to my thighs.

Another tendril shot from the ground and pressed against my throat. The pressure made my ears ache and my blood pulse wildly.

"Millie," Mother cried from where she knelt on the ground. Tears streamed down her face, guilt and terror fresh in her eyes.

The pressure against my throat tightened and my vision started to blur. I struggled to breathe and gasped for air. I could feel my eyelids getting heavy. I could feel my body panicking for life. The world was growing dim, my mother's cries fading.

"Good-bye, girl with the red medallion," the enemy murmured.

The world went dark. And in that darkness, silence.

I opened my eyes, shocked to find myself in a brilliant-white room. The world of FIGS was gone. Just . . . gone!

I gasped. Looking down at myself I saw I was free. No black cord or tendrils held me prisoner. I patted my arms and stomach. I was solid. Like a body should be.

I glanced around and saw nothing but whiteness. No FIGS. No ash. No Mother. No Soren.

Was I dead?

"No," a kind male voice said.

A middle-aged man with light-brown hair and a clean-shaven face appeared, dressed in white. He'd come from nowhere and nearly blended into the background. He smiled at me, and my soul warmed.

"Hello, Millie," he said.

Maybe it was the way his voice sounded, or the way he was looking at me, or the brilliant green of his eyes. Or maybe it was just the way I felt standing near him. But I knew who he was.

"You're the Great Teacher," I said.

"You can call me Justin. Many do," he said.

"Justin."

"Millie Maven, the girl with the red medallion. I've been looking forward to seeing you."

"Where are we?"

"In the same place you've always been. You're just seeing it differently," he said.

"I don't understand," I said.

"That's okay, the important part is why you're here."

"Why?"

"Don't you know?"

I thought back through the events that had led up to me standing in this perfectly white place with Justin.

My face fell. "Because I lost the red medallion."

"How quickly you assume the worst about yourself." Justin took a step toward me. "The red medallion is just a thing, a symbol of something you cannot lose."

I thought about his words and smiled. "Love."

"My love. A love beyond fear, which you accepted and cannot be threatened."

"Soren feels threatening," I said.

"Soren is simply fear, but you know this."

"Fear personified."

"Exactly," Justin said. "But perfect love casts out fear. It reminds you of who I am, and therefore who you are. All can remember the truth of this path if they are willing to take the journey."

"Why wouldn't they want to?"

"Fear blinds almost everyone until it is all they see.

But don't judge them; only offer them love. The same love I offered you when you were blind," Justin said.

"My mother is blind," I said.

Justin nodded. "But what you did, offering yourself in her place—love like that changes people."

"You told me to follow you," I said. "To surrender everything, and I wasn't afraid to do it."

Justin smiled broadly. "I knew you wouldn't be. That's why I chose you, Millie Maven. I knew you would be capable of love greater than the fear of death. That's the power of the red medallion. Surrender."

"That's why Dean Kyra said it had to be me," I said. The pieces were falling into place.

"She also said the purpose of FIGS was for your heart," Justin said. "The school, the medallions, the gifts—they are all ways to help you understand the power of love. Because love is the only true power there is."

Maybe I was starting to really understand. Power rose up from the floor into my feet and legs. Its warmth and strength made me feel truly alive. It spread to my waist, my back, then covered my head and made me feel full.

"I feel different," I whispered.

"You're being made new. Unless a seed falls to the grow and dies . . ." Justin started.

"It can't bear new fruit," I finished.

"You're beginning to understand."

Yes, I thought. *Through surrender I'm being made new, free of fear and filled with perfect love.*

"What happens now?" I asked.

"You finish what I called you to," Justin said. "You show them all my love."

"A love beyond fear," I said. "But how?"

"Don't be afraid, for I'm always with you and have already overcome."

"I'm not afraid," I answered honestly.

"Good. You'll know what to do when the time comes."

He turned to leave.

"Wait," I called. "Will I see you again?"

He turned back, a smile on his face. "Whenever you'd like, Millie."

"But you left. No one's seen you in a very long time."

"I never left," Justin said. "I've always been here. They just can't see me."

I thought about this for a moment. "Because fear blinds," I whispered. I looked up at Justin, who was still smiling.

"I'm so proud of you, daughter."

I smiled back, fresh tears dotting my vision.

"I love you," he said.

"I love you," I replied.

I rubbed away my tears and when I opened my eyes I was back with Soren, at FIGS, pinned against the wall, nearly out of breath.

CHAPTER TEN

Tendrils at my neck and waist held me tight to the wall, trying their best to destroy me. My mother knelt on the ground, defeated. Soren's eyes burned with hate.

I could feel the pressure against my throat. I could sense my body fighting to stay alive and recognized my frantic state of mind. But my heart was clear and filled with hope. I wasn't afraid. I wasn't uncertain. I knew who I was so deeply that even the pain Soren caused my body felt distant compared to the love that pulsed with each heartbeat.

I was different, changed forever. Transformed. Made into something new, just like Justin had said. I wasn't afraid of being defeated, because the Great Teacher, Justin, had already overcome. He was with me as I hung against the stone wall. He emboldened me.

Soren and I locked eyes and the monster saw the change in my expression. I noticed the way his shadowed face twitched with surprise and then rage. He screamed against the sky as his fog tendrils bore down on me.

But I didn't waver. He was only fear, and I was no longer afraid.

My eyes fell upon my broken medallion: still bronze, cracked into three pieces, a powerful symbol designed for my learning. I understood that now.

As it lay on the ground it started to vibrate. Quietly, the separate pieces came back together and the medallion took its original form. A soft glow formed in its center, as if a fire had been lit underneath, and the bronze metal started to shift.

Bleeding out from the glow in the middle, its former beautiful red hue spread over the medallion. It shimmered amid Soren's ash and pulsed with the power of surrender. Then it shifted again. From the center, a brilliant light flowed across the red surface and turned it a pure white, as white as the room where I'd met Justin.

White like a shining pearl radiating its own light.

Justin had said I would know what to do when it was time, and I did. That white medallion spoke to the love inside of me, and I knew I needed to get it.

But there was no way I could escape Soren's grip. My mother's whimpering reached my ears and I glanced at her.

My heart broke for her agony. I could see the depths of fear that plagued her and I wished to release her from its hold.

"Mother," I called above Soren's storm.

She looked up at me with pained eyes.

"Don't be afraid," I said. "The Great Teacher is with us, and he has already overcome."

She looked at me as if I were speaking a different language, but Soren understood.

"Shut up," he hissed.

I ignored him.

"You're just blinded by fear, Mother. But you don't have to stay blind," I said.

"Foolish girl!" Soren said. "You've lost!"

"Millie . . . I . . ."

"The love of the Great Teacher is available to all," I said. "He saved me from my own fear! He'll do the same for you."

The pressure around me tightened and my body reacted to the pain. I cried out. But the fear didn't come. I knew who I was. I kept my focus on my mother. "You can be free of all you fear. I forgive you, Mother. I love you."

Her cries multiplied as she stared up at me in amazement. I watched as the power of my words washed over her and touched something in her heart.

"All you have to do is see, Mother," I said. "Love has always been within your grasp, if you only look around and see." I knew my words were working within her heart and I prayed she discerned their message.

I saw her gaze fall on the mended white medallion. Her eyes widened. She'd seen Soren destroy it. She looked from the medallion to me and then back to the medallion. Could she feel its power the way I did? Was it touching her heart and calling her forward?

She pushed herself up quickly. I could see the tremble in her legs as she reached the medallion in four strides.

Mother snatched up the white medallion and gasped. I smiled as she looked with wonder at the pulsing symbol. A swift moment passed as she stared. I imagined what was happening inside her was similar to what had happened to me. She was feeling the love of the Great Teacher for the first time.

Love that strong changes people, Justin had said.

She was being changed.

Her eyes, filled with fresh tears, snapped up to mine. I offered her a smile and she straightened as if suddenly filled with confidence. She rushed across the stage, a powerful scream pouring from her mouth, and was at my side before Soren could assess the situation.

Mother didn't hesitate. She slammed the white medallion into my open palm, and the second it met my skin the area around the stage exploded with light. The light passed over every inch of me, and Soren's fog vanished. I floated in midair, light coming from my skin, pouring from my fingers, ignited in my eyes. I felt it run through my blood, pulse with my heart, sing with my soul.

And then it all collapsed back into the medallion and I landed on the stone stage, both feet underneath me.

But the medallion in my right hand felt like it had changed. I looked down to see not a medallion, but a brilliant white sword! I was holding the hilt and its blade hung to the ground, buzzing with power. But of course! It was the sword of truth, a white sword that was the word of the Great Teacher. He was using his power through me, because he was always with me. Just as he had promised.

The white medallion had thrown Soren off the stage.

He was lying on the ground twenty feet away, back in human form. He struggled to his feet and faced me, his hood knocked off, his pale skin visibly striped with dark veins.

I approached, dragging the white sword, unmoved by the sight of him. He was just fear after all. And I was standing with the Great Teacher's sword of truth. The truth that cast out all fear.

A thought pulsed in my brain. Soren was only shadow. All the tendrils of fog floating in the air, crawling on the ground, descending from the clouds, wrapping around FIGS—they were really just shadows.

"I will destroy you, Millie Maven!" Soren screamed. He lifted his hands to hurl attacks at me.

I realized the best way to be rid of shadows is to turn on the lights. Light dispels darkness. Love casts out fear because fear is just a shadow.

The world slowed and I saw the massive collection of fog tendrils headed for me. I took the hilt of the white sword in both hands, feeling the light of the Great Teacher pulsing under my skin, and I lifted it up, blade pointing straight down. With all my might I slammed the blade into the earth at my feet and spoke with unshakable authority.

"No!" I cried.

The tendrils froze in midair and Soren's face filled with terror.

"Light casts out all shadows," I said. A brilliant ray of light came out of the sword in every direction and seared the air. The light, which was the word of the Great Teacher, streaked through the tendrils of fear and deception and erased them from the sky and ground. It blasted through Soren, and he released a horrified scream. His form flaked away in dark ashes, which turned to dust. And then he was gone.

But the light wasn't finished. It sought out all of the darkness, destroying it until every last one of Soren's lies were gone. And when all traces of the darkness were gone, the light collapsed back into the palm of my hand.

I looked down, breathing hard. Instead of the sword I held the medallion—pure white with a sword engraved on one side.

The world went still. I took several deep breaths as my eyes scanned what they could see. There were no more tendrils of darkness, no dark clouds. The wind was breezy and warm.

But the destruction Soren had done remained. FIGS was still ash and dust.

Soft whimpering drew my attention behind me. I

turned to see my mother, numb and crying. My heart broke. I walked to her and grasped her hands.

Her eyes jumped to mine and I could see the disbelief behind them.

"It's okay, Mother," I said softly. "Soren is gone."

Fresh tears collected in her eyes. She dropped to her knees and clung to me into a tight hug. "I thought he was going to . . ." She couldn't finish.

I returned her embrace and felt the warmth of love pass through us. "He couldn't have," I said. "The Great Teacher was with me. There was never anything to be afraid of."

She pulled back and gently tucked my hair behind my ear. "I'm so sorry, Millie. I've been so cruel."

"It's alright," I said. "I understand now how fear and love work. I've seen the Great Teacher, Mother. I know him."

"I felt him too," she whispered, looking down at the white medallion in my hand. "I heard his voice. I didn't know such love was possible." Again her raw emotions threatened her ability to speak.

I placed my hand on her cheek. "It is," I said, drawing her eyes back to mine. "The Great Teacher loves everyone. He made a way for all to experience his love. To let go of their fears. And to love one another the same way he loves us." I smiled at her. "The way I love you."

Her eyes lit with wonder and then flashed with guilt. I knew she was still dealing with all she had done, and it would take time to love herself the way I did. But that was fine. I wouldn't judge her. I would instead offer her love and help her remember who she really was.

"How could you ever forgive me?" she whispered.

"I already have," I said and leaned forward to kiss her forehead.

Another wave of sobs shook her shoulders and I wrapped her in a loving embrace. For a few minutes we stayed there on the stone stage, letting the power of forgiveness and love redeem what had been broken. And I knew we would never be the same.

My mother pulled back and her eyes widened at something behind me. I turned to see Rebecca entering the amphitheater and joy filled my chest.

The beautiful woman smiled at us as she joined us on the stage. I released Mother and walked to wrap my arms around Rebecca's waist. She chuckled and hugged me back. I pulled away and glanced back at my mother. Her mouth was slightly ajar and her eyes wide.

I would have been surprised too if I were seeing an angel for the first time. That's what Rebecca had to be.

My guardian angel, sent from the Great Teacher to love and protect me.

"Oh, Millie," Rebecca said. "You've done so well."

A happy chirping sounded overhead, and the small blue bird Paxaro swooped down from the clouds and landed on Rebecca's shoulder. He sang in her ear and she nodded.

"Paxaro thinks you may be his favorite student ever to come through FIGS," Rebecca said.

I reached up to pet the bird. "Well, you're my favorite bird of all time." He sang in response and took back to the sky to fly about the amphitheater. I followed him with my eyes and was reminded how demolished it still was.

"I thought that if I destroyed Soren, then all of his destruction would be set right," I said.

"There's still healing to be done here," Rebecca said. "Don't worry, Millie, the Great Teacher restores all who seek him."

She grabbed my hands. "There's one more thing you must remember: What you have learned here is for your world and the great struggle you still have to face when you return."

"Great struggle? What do you mean?" I asked, unnerved.

"Everything will be made clear, but your journey is not over, sweet girl. Promise me you will remember to love in the face of fear. To forgive even what may feel unforgivable. Remember the words and truth of the Great Teacher. Can you promise me that?"

I nodded with a smile, still unsure what she might mean. But I wasn't afraid. I knew the Great Teacher would be with me.

Rebecca placed a kiss on the top of my head. Then she moved to my mother, who still looked stunned.

Rebecca took my mother's hands into her own and they stared at one another. Rebecca smiled and brought my mother's left hand upward, leaned forward, and kissed my mother's knuckles ever so softly.

Mother's bottom lip quivered and her eyes misted. Then Rebecca released Mother's hands and turned toward the stone wall where we had been pinned.

I looked up too and noticed a scorched image on the stone. A cross. I walked to Rebecca's side. She stared up at the image and smiled.

"A powerful reminder of the Great Teacher's sacrifice," she said. "This is the place where he showed us all that even death is a shadow." She laid a hand on my shoulder and gave me a wink. "The world will try to snuff out the light the Great Teacher has lit in you with the shadows of fear. Remember, he is always with you, working through you. Never forget."

"I won't," I said. How could I after all I had seen?

She nodded and turned to leave.

"Will I ever see you again?" I asked.

Rebecca's eyes darted to my mother and then back to me. "You will always have me, Millie Maven." With that she walked off the stage and into the dead forest behind the amphitheater.

CHAPTER ELEVEN

I watched Rebecca until I couldn't see her anymore, then turned back to my mother. Rebecca had said there was still healing to be done. I wondered what she meant as I took Mother's hand.

I led her off the stage and into the center of the amphitheater. Paxaro flew down from the sky and landed on one of the stone statues. He chirped and cocked his neck to the side, staring at me.

My eyes studied the small statue and curiosity nipped at my brain. I didn't remember seeing it before. I glanced around and noticed there were several more statues than I remembered. Actually, as I checked more carefully, I decided there were nearly twice as many.

I released Mother's hand.

"Where are you going?"

"I need to check something," I replied and walked to

the statue where Paxaro was perched. As I approached, he rose into the clouds. I immediately saw the difference between this statue and the ones that were in the garden when Dean Kyra led us here. This child wasn't in a joyful posture but looked stern. I glanced at the other stone figures that also seemed out of place.

The original statues all shared one trait: joy. The stone figure before me looked . . . trapped. My mind tumbled over a possibility that was taking shape in my brain.

The figure before me stood straight, long hair hanging down over both shoulders. My heart skipped. It almost looked like . . .

Doris.

The white medallion pulsed in my palm. It was glowing, and I raised it up toward the stone Doris. Carefully, I placed it against the statue's chest and held my breath.

A second passed, then warmth spread down my arm and light started to penetrate the stone. The statue vibrated and its surface cracked. The steady but powerful wind I often felt with the Great Teacher's presence whirled around me and surrounded the stone figure.

I stepped back as the wind formed a small funnel of light and swirled around the statue. A moment later it thinned and vanished. What it left behind wasn't stone. Doris stood before me, gasping for deep breaths of air, her eyes wide with wonder.

Shocked and thrilled, I glanced around. The students were here! They were trapped in stone, but they were here. I turned my gaze back to Doris. The look on her face stopped me from rushing off to free the others.

Sadness ruled all her features. "I did this," she whispered, taking in all the destruction.

"No," I said. "Soren did this."

"I let him use me," Doris said, tears in her eyes.

I grabbed her hand. "We were all blinded by fear."

"Not you," she said.

"Yes, I was. Maybe worse than anyone. But the Great Teacher showed me a different way."

She dropped her eyes to her feet and sniffed back her tears. "I don't want to be afraid anymore."

"You don't have to be," I opened her palm and placed the white medallion in her hand. "The Great Teacher made a way for us all. You just have to see it." I closed her fingers around the medallion and felt the love rush from my hand to Doris's. She gasped as it worked up through her fingers and into her arm.

She closed her eyes. I watched her body relax

into the love I knew she was feeling. I waited as truth washed over her and the Great Teacher showed her his perfect love.

When she opened her eyes and looked at me, there was something new in them. A light of clarity. She smiled and tears of joy fell down her cheeks.

"I can feel him, hear him," Doris whispered. "And I don't feel afraid."

I yanked the girl into a hug. She giggled and hugged me back, a deep connection forming between us. When I pulled back she was holding my gaze kindly.

"I'm so sorry, Millie," she said.

"It's okay. I'm sorry too."

Doris looked down at the white medallion, bright and glowing in her palm. "Is my fear really gone?" she asked softly.

"I think so, but a wise woman told me once that life is a cycle of remembering and forgetting."

"What do you do when you forget?" Doris asked.

"I listen for the voice of the Great Teacher. Once you see him, once he's in your heart, he is always with you, Doris. You just have to listen to the voice of love instead of fear."

She nodded. "I never want this feeling to end. For the first time I feel . . ." She thought about her words, biting the inside of her bottom lip. Then she smiled. "Loved."

"You are, Doris. So very much. I think that's the point of FIGS. To teach us each about the power of love."

"Like Dean Kyra's always saying," Doris started, "it's really about our hearts."

Hearing her name made me wonder about the faculty. There weren't any adult-sized statues here, so where could they be?

"Friends?" Doris asked with a shrug.

I turned my attention back to her and shook my head. "No, we're sisters now."

Her smiled grew and she giggled. I glanced to the side and saw another stone figure that resembled her, but male. *Dash*, I thought. I pointed at him.

She walked away toward the statue and placed the white medallion at its chest, as I had done with her. The same powerful light funnel swirled around the figure and broke it open, freeing Dash from its clutches.

He looked at Doris and without a word wrapped her tightly in a hug. "I love you, sister," he said. And right before my eyes, in a matter of seconds, the twins released any judgment of each other.

Doris offered the medallion back to me and I moved to the next statue. It held Boomer. The pudgy boy squeezed me tightly once he was free, then walked with me as I freed the others. The white medallion was liberating them from their stone prisons, and the love of the Great Teacher was working through them. Each student changed and offered one another unconditional forgiveness.

Mac was the last stone figure. The swirl of light had hardly disappeared when she launched herself at me in a hug and nearly knocked me off my feet. I laughed and held my friend close.

"Oh, Millie," Mac said. "I knew you could do it. I knew it would all be alright."

"Thanks for having my back," I said.

"Always," she said.

Boomer gasped. "Millie, look!" He was pointing at the ground. I looked down and saw the destruction was starting to shift. Light bursting forth from all corners of the amphitheater was bringing the dark, dead land back to life. The flowers bloomed, the grass sprouted, and the trees grew new leaves. Birds and butterflies and bees returned, and within minutes the Children's Garden was reborn.

All the students giggled and jumped about, excitement filling the air. I glanced up and saw him standing on the stage in white. Justin. His piercing blue eyes locked with mine.

He smiled at me and I felt his love fill the air.

"I can feel him," Mac said. "The Great Teacher is here with us."

She was looking right at him, and I realized I was still the only one who could see him but they all knew he was there. Maybe it was because I'd met him before, or because I was holding the white medallion. But there he was, where he had always been.

"He's always with us," I said.

Boomer threw his arm around my shoulders. "You really are special, Millie Maven."

Justin threw me a wink and I smiled so big it hurt my cheeks.

Mother was standing to the side, watching us all in wonder. Could she feel the Great Teacher like the rest of us? I hoped she could. I hoped she knew how powerful his love was.

She felt me watching and turned her gaze to me. Her smile warmed my already bursting heart.

"I wonder if FIGS is back?" Mac asked. She pulled me toward the arch. "Come on."

I followed, Boomer at my side, urging others to come. As a group with my mother at the back, we wandered from the amphitheater and toward the school. As we moved, the light of the Great Teacher moved with us. The ground under our feet, the forest at our side, the world around us turned from death to life.

The Great Teacher was working through us, restoring and making everything new, just as he had done with each of us. Students swiped their hands over patches of earth and flowers bloomed. Trees regained their foliage. Bushes turned back to green. It was wondrous.

The notion of individual gifts, some better than others, left us as we all used the gift of life from the Great Teacher. We crested the hill and watched as the light spread wide in front of us and restored the grand FIGS lawn.

The tall oaks leafed out, the grass beneath greened up, and the gravel path reformed all the way to the foundation of the school.

We approached as a group, staring at the desolate structure. We stepped up onto the foundation and walked to where the grand staircase would have been.

The white medallion glowed in my hand and I stepped out from the group.

Show them my love, daughter. Show them all.

I dropped to a knee and placed the white medallion on the ground. It vibrated with power, and light spread out from all around it. The light rushed across the damaged floor, up over the few remaining walls, and out in all directions.

The warm wind flowed over us and around us as the destroyed parts of FIGS began to mend. I stood and felt the love of the Great Teacher so heavy in the air that it was like swimming through his pools.

We watched as the light reformed everything Soren's darkness had shattered. Within minutes, FIGS was back in its original state. Well, not quite in its original state, because it was different. It looked the same but it was new. Knitted back together in light through love.

Doris grabbed my hand.

"I can feel the Great Teacher everywhere," she said. "Thank you for showing him to me."

Before I could respond, Mac gasped.

"Look," she said.

I turned my head and saw Dean Kyra and the professors coming into the entry hall through the double doors. Their faces filled with warmth as they approached us. The students mumbled excitedly and we embraced the professors, everyone talking at once.

"Where were you?"

"What happened?"

"Can you feel the Great Teacher?"

"You should have seen what Millie did!"

"She defeated Soren!"

Dean Kyra smiled and raised her hands for quiet.

"Calm down, students. One question at a time."

"What happened to you and the professors?" Mac asked.

"We were trapped in the dungeons," Dean Kyra said. "Until the light from the Great Teacher swept over this place and set us free."

"Will Soren come back? Will he be part of the third trial?" Dash asked.

She paused and smiled broadly. "No," she said. "You've already completed the third trial."

"That was the third trial?" Boomer asked.

"Much different from any we've seen, but yes. The third trial has always been about surrendering everything to love, because only when you surrender to love can fear be seen as the lie that it is. Perfect love casts out fear."

"The love of the Great Teacher," Doris said.

Dean Kyra smiled. "Yes, the most powerful love of all."

"I can feel him now, with me," Mac said.

"So can I," Doris said.

Mumbles of agreement sounded from all the students.

"We all can," I said.

Dean Kyra's eyes filled with tears. "Yes."

"He has always been here," I said. "We were just too blind to see him."

Professor Alexandria moved toward me, her eyes bright with light. She placed her hand on my shoulder. The rest of the group waited as she looked me in the eye. "I was wrong about you, Miss Maven. I was blinded by my own fear, and for that I'm sorry. Thank you for believing in your call. I can see now that the Great Teacher has always been with me."

The not-so-grumpy teacher hugged me tightly and I thought my heart might burst. Professor Alexandria released me and stepped back. I saw Professor Gabriel standing a few yards away, smiling like a fool. He threw me a wink. Like Dean Kyra, he had always known more than he let on. He'd let me discover it on my own.

Maybe that's the only way to learn, I thought. I threw him a wink back and he chuckled. I'm not sure I was very good at winking.

"You have all learned everything we can teach you," Dean Kyra said. "Your hearts are ready to return to the worlds from which you came."

"Wait, we have to leave FIGS?" Mac asked.

"Yes, Miss Spitzer. This is always the way."

The room fell quiet as everyone thought about what that meant: Leaving the teachers we had come to love.

Leaving the school that had taught us so much. Leaving each other.

"When?" Doris asked.

Dean Kyra exhaled and nodded. "Now."

"Can't we stay a little longer?" Mac asked.

"Your lives outside of FIGS are waiting," Dean Kyra said. "That's where the real trial begins. You cannot delay. Besides, we have more students coming and we have to prepare."

"Will we remember each other and FIGS when we're gone?" Boomer asked.

"Your memories will fade with time," Dean Kyra said. "It happens quickly so that you can focus on where you are and not on where you have been."

Some of the whispers sounded worried. I glanced back to see Mother standing in the corner watching, unsure what she was supposed to do. She felt my eyes and glanced up at me. I smiled and she returned the gesture.

I turned back to the group. Many of the kids were looking at me for guidance. I looped my arm through Mac's as she had done to me a hundred times over our time here at FIGS.

"We're ready," I said. I looked around at the friends I'd come to love so dearly. "We may be leaving, but we'll never really be apart. We're connected through the Great Teacher, so you'll always live in my heart."

Mac squeezed my arm. "Sisters."

Doris took my free arm and did the same. "Sisters."

"And brothers," Boomer said from behind. The group chuckled and moved in closer together.

"Family," I said.

"Family!" they all cheered.

"We're so proud of you all," Dean Kyra said. "We'll never forget you. May the Great Teacher guide you always."

We cheered again and I knew in my heart he always would.

Chapter Twelve

The professors collected our medallions before we left, explaining that in our world the gifts we received at FIGS would no longer exist. But no one seemed disappointed about that. Our hearts had changed. Love was the real power we would take back home.

I hugged every professor as they heaped each of us with praise for all we'd accomplished. Saying good-bye to Dean Kyra was the hardest. The thought of never hearing her wisdom or seeing her kind eyes again made my heart hurt.

As the students followed Riggs and Chaplin out the school doors, Dean Kyra held something out to me.

"Here," she said. "You should have this." It was the white medallion.

"I can take this with me?"

"The Great Teacher gave it to you, so it should stay with you," she said. "Never, never forget the perfect love of the Great Teacher." She kissed the top of my head. "You'll always be in my heart, Millie Maven."

"And you in mine," I replied.

I rushed to join the others, who were already a distance from the school.

Your lives outside of FIGS are waiting. That's where the real trial begins.

Dean Kyra's words reminded me of Rebecca's. Something else was coming. Something I still had to face. I hoped I could remember all I'd learned.

When our group made it to the tree line, I looked over my shoulder at FarPointe Institute and gasped. It was gone, hidden behind the invisible wall that kept its secrets.

Mother was at my side. "What happened to it?"

"We just can't see it, that's all. But it will always be with us."

"Like the Great Teacher," my mother said.

Surprised, I looked at her. I hadn't even thought about that and it made me smile. "Yeah."

She took my hand. "Let's go home."

Riggs and Chaplin, who'd been locked in the basement with the professors, led us all the way to the ocean. The boat we'd arrived on four weeks ago was moored to a pier on the shore.

We quickly boarded and set sail. Dean Kyra had told us before we left FIGS that after we fell asleep on the boat, we would wake up in the place we'd left. Which meant none of us wanted to fall asleep.

Instead, we celebrated. The boat was stocked with food and lanterns, so we ate and drank, chatted and laughed. Dash turned a bucket over and started playing a rhythm Professor Tomas had taught him, and then we danced.

I introduced my mother to everyone. Though shy and quiet at first, within a couple hours she was laughing with the rest of us. Sleeping mats came out as exhaustion took over. One by one people said final good-byes and slipped into sleep.

Mac, Boomer, and I were the last three awake.

"And then there were only three," Mac said, looking at the sleeping bodies. Even Mother had drifted off.

"The original three," Boomer said. "Seems appropriate."

"Can you believe how much we've been through?" Mac asked.

"It's been . . ." I was at a loss for words.

"Awesomesauce," Mac said.

I giggled softly and nodded. We were quiet for a moment. I wondered if they were as tired as I was, and Boomer's wide yawn confirmed my suspicions. Our time was coming to an end.

"Do you remember when Doris melted the orb I found, like on day three?" Boomer said.

"I thought the Elites were the worst," Mac said.

"And now Dash is one of my best friends," Boomer murmured.

I smiled. The twins slept on the other side of the deck. We really had been on an amazing adventure together. Mac launched into another memory and for the next thirty minutes we reminisced, trying to etch the memories into our brains.

"I know Dean Kyra said we would forget this place," Boomer started. "But I'm hoping I don't. I can't imagine ever forgetting the two coolest girls I've ever meet."

I smiled at him and nodded. Maybe we wouldn't forget. Though the things Dean Kyra said usually came to pass.

Boomer was the first to go. With heavy eyes we said our good-byes and I saw tears spring to Mac's eyes. There would never be another Boomer. And then it was only Mac and me.

We held hands in silence and I could feel sleep

coming for me. I didn't want to go. I couldn't stand the thought of never seeing Mac again.

"Promise me you'll never forget how special you are, Millie Maven," Mac whispered. I saw a tear run down her cheek.

"Promise me you'll never forget how much I love you," I said back. My own tears collected.

She nodded and sniffed. "You're my best friend."

I nodded back, feeling my tears fall. "You're mine too."

Mac smiled. "I'm really tired, but I don't want to go to sleep."

"It's okay, Mac," I said, trying to offer her comfort. "You'll always have me. Remember that."

"I wish I could go back with you," she said.

"But your world needs you. It needs your heart and strength."

"Do you think we'll ever meet again?" she asked.

I smiled and shrugged. "I don't know. You're the one who gets feelings about these kinds of things."

She chuckled. "Then I say yes. We'll see each other again."

"We'll see each other again," I repeated.

She yawned, then I did too. I leaned my head back against the side of the boat and Mac leaned her head on my shoulder.

"Don't fall asleep, Millie," Mac whispered with her eyes closed.

I closed my eyes just to rest them. "I won't," I said. But then I did.

✦

Priscilla opened her eyes. A moment of comfort passed before the memories of all that had transpired returned. She shot up from where she was lying and saw she was in her bed at the mansion in Paradise. Her heart raced. Her clothes were damp. The white silk stuck to her skin like a bandage.

Her mind tumbled over itself as she tried to make sense of the events replaying behind her eyes. The things she'd seen and experienced couldn't be possible. Had it been a dream? Had it been a nightmare? She threw herself out of bed and rushed from her room, across the hallway to her husband's bedroom. It was empty. Right. He was gone. A weeklong business trip.

What day was it? What time was it? Had she actually been dragged through a pool to another world by . . . she looked down the hallway as an image of the sweet girl passed through her mind. Millie.

Her heart broke and warmed almost in sync. She was taken aback for a moment at the emotions that rose in her. If it had all been a dream, then why did she feel so different? The emotional charge of her experience at FIGS rushed back. Priscilla nearly dropped to her knees.

Shame and guilt parried with deep love, and a desire to protect Millie at all costs filled her gut. For so many years she had dumped her own self-loathing onto the innocent child. For so long she had hated Millie because she had hated her sister. She had hated herself. For so long she'd blamed the world for the pain it caused her, but really she was just afraid of her own inadequacies.

Priscilla walked down the hallway on shaky legs. Millie had offered her forgiveness in the face of unforgivable actions, because of the perfect love she'd found through the Great Teacher. Priscilla would never have believed such a love existed had she not felt it herself. Had she not seen it in Millie's eyes. Heard it in her words.

Had she not seen Rebecca.

The wonder of real love had worked its way into Priscilla's heart, and she was experiencing it as never before. She stopped mid stride and smiled, tears filling her eyes. How long had she gone without knowing something so wondrous? She didn't even feel like the same woman. She needed to find Millie.

Priscilla quickened her steps down the stairs, all the way to the first floor. She rounded the corner and nearly crashed into Martha.

"Sorry, ma'am, I . . ." Martha took in Priscilla's appearance and looked at her curiously. "Are you alright? Your clothes—"

"Have you seen Millie?" Priscilla asked.

"She's returned? I didn't . . . I didn't know," Martha said.

"What day is it?"

"Wednesday," the old woman answered cautiously.

Not even eight hours had passed since she'd been taken through the pool. Was that even possible?

Martha was looking at her with great concern. Priscilla noticed the dark circles under her eyes, the worried lines in her face. Empathy flooded her. A dozen questions crashed inside her brain.

How could she have been so cruel to this poor mother?

How could she have exploited her sick daughter?

Was her daughter okay?

Was Abby going to live?

Had she ever asked?

"Ma'am . . ." Martha started.

Priscilla took Martha's hands in her own. "I'm so sorry for all the suffering I've put you and Abby through. Please forgive me."

Martha's face went white and her mouth dropped open.

"Whatever Abby needs, I will help," Priscilla said. "No strings attached. How was her appointment?"

Again, Martha just stared for a long moment. She cleared her throat.

"Her scans were better," Martha said. "But it's a long road ahead."

"That's good news. I promise to be there, if you want, the whole time."

Martha shook her head, eyes still perplexed. "I don't understand."

"I've been cruel. I used your misfortune to manipulate you into servitude, and I see how wrong I was. I don't expect forgiveness, but I promise to do my best to try to make things right," Priscilla said.

"What happened to you?" Martha asked.

"She met the Great Teacher," a small voice said behind the ladies.

Priscilla spun around and saw Millie walking down the last few steps, her face bright.

"Millie," Martha said. "You're back."

In three long strides Priscilla reached the girl and pulled her into a hug. "You're here," she whispered.

Millie returned her hug. "Of course! Where else would I be?"

"I'll get some breakfast ready then," Martha said.

"Thank you," Priscilla said, glancing back at the still-shocked woman. Martha rushed away toward the kitchen.

Millie's eyes were aglow with love and power. They sparked and drew Priscilla in. She just held them for a long moment.

"It's okay, Mother," Millie said. "We're home."

The girl said *home* like she believed it, though this had never been the kind of home she deserved. It had been a prison, and yet there Millie stood, filled with optimism and hope, void of worry and fear. She wasn't the same either.

Another image of Rebecca crossed her mind and broke Priscilla's heart. Her eyes filled with tears and she watched sorrow flash across Millie's face.

"Don't cry," the girl said. "We're back, but the Great Teacher's love is still with us. Now we can love each other better. Be mother and daughter for real."

Priscilla smiled and tucked a stray hair gently behind Millie's ear. A tear slipped down Priscilla's cheek and she smiled. "I would love that. That's all I've ever wanted."

"We can have it," Millie said. "I love you."

"I love you too, sweet girl, but this is not where you belong."

Millie's eyes shadowed with curiosity. "What do you mean?"

Priscilla wiped her cheeks clear. "I'll show you. I need you to go pack up all your things. We're going on a trip, just you and me."

"Really? Where?"

"I'll tell you when we get there," Priscilla said. "Now, go quickly. We'll leave as soon as we eat."

Millie smiled and rushed back up the stairs toward the top floor. Priscilla watched the small girl go, her heart breaking. For a moment she second-guessed her choice. After just learning to love, how was she supposed to do this? But then a warm peace passed over her, like wind from nowhere, and she knew it was love itself calling her to action. She knew what needed to happen next.

CHAPTER THIRTEEN

Mother and I traveled for more than fifteen hours. We crossed the states of Utah and Nevada, stopped overnight in a small motel along the interstate, and ended up in California on the morning of the second day.

Although a long drive, Mother and I had a blast. We talked and laughed. I told her every story I could think of from my time at FIGS, as she listened with fascination. She questioned the existence of FIGS on more than one occasion.

"Could it really have happened? Maybe it was all in my head," she would suggest. "But I had been there too," I would remind her. "We couldn't have had the exact same dream. Right? Aggie said everything that happened at FIGS was as real as everything that happened here."

It had to be real. But in the moments of silence, I found myself wondering if it even mattered. What was real, beyond a shadow of a doubt, was the love of the Great Teacher. I could feel his love with me constantly.

As the hours stretched, our memories grew fuzzy. My mother forgot first. One moment she was nodding when I said the Great Teacher's name, and the next she was asking me who the Great Teacher was.

Dean Kyra had told me that would happen . . . or maybe someone else gave me that idea? I couldn't remember and I knew my own memories were changing. The blurriness worsened as we traveled and soon we had little to talk about.

Mother told me stories about being a little girl and some of the things she'd struggled with. I began to understand why she'd dug such deep caverns of fear and how much pain she was learning to release.

All the while, I wondered where she could possibly be taking me. She wouldn't tell me, no matter how many times I asked.

I watched signs carefully and deciphered we were in San Diego when Mother finally parked the car along a residential street. Small, brightly painted homes were lined up in both directions. Most had white shutters and small front lawns. Tall palm trees grew along both sides of the street and the sun was bright, warming the air even in the middle of December.

I jumped out of the car and shut the passenger door. I felt nervous as I walked around the back of our car to stand with Mother on the sidewalk. Through the back windshield I saw my single black suitcase filled with some new clothes Mother had bought for me. For some reason I didn't have any at the Colorado house. I wondered how long we would be here.

My mother stared across the street at a little blue house with white shutters and a bright-yellow front door. A short white fence bordered the front lawn, and a large collection of sunflowers bloomed from planters on either side of the front porch.

"Do you know who lives here?" I asked.

Mother's eyes looked worried and pained, but she forced a grin and nodded. She opened the back door and grabbed my suitcase.

"Come on," she said, offering me her hand.

I took it and we walked across the quiet street to the yard's gate, then through. As if on cue, the yellow door popped open and a beautiful, familiar-looking woman walked out onto the front porch. She wore a wide-brimmed sunhat and had gardening gloves tucked into the front pocket of her denim overalls. A box of gardening tools dangled from her right hand. She looked so familiar, and the name "Rebecca" popped into my head, but I couldn't place her.

The woman glanced up at us and froze. Her eyes locked with Mother's, confusion playing across her face.

"Priscilla?" she said. Her voice was warm and comforting as my brain tried to understand how I knew her face.

"Hello, Becky," Mother said. She set my black suitcase on the ground.

"Becky?" I whispered. "Your sister?" My words died as reality crashed into my mind. If this was Becky, her sister, then she was my . . .

My eyes flew up to Mother, who was staring down at me, tears running down her cheeks. "Millie," she said. "I'd like you to meet your mother. Your real mother."

I turned back to the beautiful gardener and watched as her expression turned from confusion, to disbelief, to recognition.

"Millie," the woman whispered, her bottom lip trembling. Her eyes lit with joy as she dropped the box she was holding and rushed across the yard to me. I felt a beat of fear and uncertainty as she pulled me into her arms. My mind said she was a stranger.

But the moment I was in her embrace, my fear faded. My heart knew who was holding me. I melted into her and started to cry. Becca was weeping as well as she pulled back from me, shaking her head in disbelief. She wiped the tears from my cheeks, felt my skin, ran her fingers through my hair as if checking to make sure I was real.

"Millie," she cried, tears dripping over her lips and off her chin. "I don't understand. How?"

"Mom?" I said. "You're my real mom?"

"Oh, baby," she said and yanked me back into her arms. "It's me. It's really me. And it's really you. I thought you were . . ."

She pulled back again. "I never stopped thinking about you. Wishing for you. Wondering what you look like." She smiled and chuckled, her eyes washing over me. "You're even more beautiful than I imagined."

I couldn't find words to express what was happening in my heart, so I only smiled and hugged her again. My real mom! I didn't understand and didn't care. I only wanted to stay in her arms forever.

After more long moments of holding one another, Becca looked at Priscilla. "How? Where? I don't even know the right question to ask."

Priscilla had stepped away from us and looked like

she might crumple from shame. "I'm so sorry," she whispered. "I did a terrible thing to you. To you both."

The story fell from Priscilla's lips in rapid chunks. She had kidnapped me from the hospital after the accident that had killed my father. She'd hated my mother for abandoning her. She'd hated my mother for being able to bear children when she could not.

Priscilla's words came through heavy sobs and self-loathing as my real mother stared in shock. I felt my own anger rage.

She'd taken me! From my mother! From my life!

She'd stolen what should have been mine.

Hot, angry tears gathered as my real mother continued to look shell-shocked, and Priscilla continued her sorrowful rambling.

She and Augustus had paid the Paradise sheriff and hospital head to tell Becca that her daughter and husband had died. She'd taken everything from Becca because she herself felt so worthless and angry.

She was so sorry, she kept saying. So sorry.

So sorry.

A warm wind swept over my shoulders, and I felt the presence of peace. And from within I heard a voice.

Daughter, let me tell you the ways I love you.

Perfect love filled my heart. Aunt Priscilla's voice

faded until only the voice within remained.

Do not resist when evil comes against you; rather, love as I have loved. Such love casts out fear. Follow me in love.

I wasn't sure how I knew, but I was certain I'd journeyed a long way to get here and had learned about love for this moment. Love was greater than fear. I had experienced this love, and it was now a small voice singing inside my heart. The voice of love.

My mother's mouth opened and her eyes started to darken. I grasped her hand. She looked at me, tears slipping down her cheeks.

"It's okay, Mom," I whispered. "I'm here now."

Her face twisted with so many emotions. Fear, anger, pain. Relief, love, joy. I could see it was too much for her brain to process right now. It would take time, but I would be there to hold her hand and love her through it.

I squeezed her hand and she smiled, her joy overwhelming all else she felt.

Priscilla had stopped talking and was sniffling. My mom pulled me close.

"We can discuss this all later," Becca said to Priscilla. "Right now I'm just happy to have my daughter home."

"I love you, Mom," I said through my own tears.

"Oh, my precious Millie," she said, holding me tight, kissing my face over and over. "I love you too."

I cried more tears of happiness as it all started to settle into my bones. The voice of love was strong within me. I could feel love for my aunt Priscilla, even after all she'd done. I knew I was called to love in this way. It felt like love itself was holding me there in the yard, and I felt so full I thought my heart couldn't take it.

"My daughter," my mom whispered. "Home."

For the first time I felt like I really was home.

✦

Aunt Priscilla slipped away while my mom and I held each other on the lawn. It was December 19.

More details of my history came out later during phone conversations between my mom and aunt. Many I didn't understand and wasn't privy to, because my mom wanted to protect me.

At times I could tell she was angry and thought maybe I should be angry too. The last twelve years of my life could have been spent with my real mom. But my heart had been changed by love, and I knew Aunt Priscilla was different now. I wasn't sure how, but she had been changed. She had brought me home.

And I remembered, though I couldn't say where I'd learned it, that one of the great lessons was not to judge, but rather to love as I had been loved. I knew this love so deeply I suspected it had always been with me.

I talked about the love with my mom, and she told me it sounded like lessons from a teacher she knew in her heart. Yeshua. I encouraged my mom to forgive her sister, and I knew with time she would.

I had my first real Christmas, with cookie decorating and gift wrapping and presents, for me! They were perfect, but I would have been happy without it all because I had my mom back.

We built blanket forts in the living room. I helped her garden. We cooked together, went shopping together, and every night she read her favorite book to me, a story about a magic wardrobe and the children who traveled through it to a fantastic place.

Something about the story felt familiar, as if I knew exactly what those kids were going through. Maybe my mom was just a really good storyteller. She was everything a girl could hope for. Warm, funny, kind, a good listener, attentive. Sometimes when I fell asleep, I was afraid I'd wake up and learn she was just a dream. And every morning when I woke up in my new room, I was filled with so much joy I thought I'd burst.

Three weeks after I arrived, I woke up, dressed, ate a

special pancake breakfast, and headed to the bus stop. It was the first day back from winter break at Roger Peak Middle School, and my first day of real school ever.

I was nervous and excited as I climbed the yellow bus's stairs and headed for an empty row halfway down the aisle. I sat as the driver instructed and held my new red backpack in my lap. Red was my favorite color these days. It felt . . . special, though I couldn't quite place why.

I took out the drawing pad and pencils Mom had given to me for Christmas and sketched the beautiful garden that kept showing up in my dreams. I couldn't remember ever being there, but I saw it so clearly that I wondered if I might have and just couldn't place where.

A few minutes later the bus made another stop and others got on. I kept my eyes on my art until a voice disrupted my focus.

"Anyone sitting here?" the voice said.

I looked up to see a small girl with short, fiery red hair and excited brown eyes. Something pricked the back of my mind, then faded. I offered the girl a smile and shook my head. She slid in beside me and extended her hand for me to shake.

"Name's Mackenzie," she said. "But my friends call me Mac."

"Millie," I said.

"You're new here, right?"

"Yeah, it's my first day."

"Good thing I found you," she said. "First days can be hard without a friend."

I smiled. I liked her already.

She squinted her eyes and scrunched her nose at me.

"What?" I asked.

"I don't know. Something about you seems . . ."

"Like we've met before?"

Her eyes lit with excitement, then she giggled and I did the same. Sitting beside her felt comfortable and familiar. It was a strange way to feel after meeting someone for the first time.

"Cool necklace," Mac said.

I glanced down and pulled the white medallion out so she could get a better look. I never took it off. It was my favorite possession.

"Where'd you get it?" Mac asked.

The details were kind of blurry. "In a cave, back behind the house I used to live in."

"A cave? Awesomesauce. You know, they say that things found in caves are special."

"Really?" I asked.

"Well, I actually haven't heard anyone say that

exactly, but they should."

I giggled again and she looped her arm through mine.

"I like you, Millie. I get the feeling we're going to be best friends. And I'm known to get feelings about these sorts of things."

I believed her. "I'd like that."

We rode the bus chatting about our lives and what might come at school. My new life was before me, filled with love, and friends, and family. My white medallion hung over my heart. No matter what came next, everything was going to be perfect.

THE END